Ghost Stories of Delaware County

Charles J. Adams III

EXETER HOUSE BOOKS

Ghost Stories of Delaware County

©2005 Charles J. Adams III

All rights reserved under the U.S. Copyright Law.
No portion of this book may be reproduced
in any form whatsoever, except with written
permission from the publisher.

For information, contact:
EXETER HOUSE BOOKS
P.O. Box 8134
Reading, PA 19603
www.ExeterHouseBooks.com

FIRST EDITION 2005
PRINTED IN THE UNITED STATES OF AMERICA

ISBN 1-880683-21-0

TABLE OF CONTENTS

Preface.. 1
Introduction 8
The Sneezing Nun... 20
The Lady in Blue..26
Legends Live at Linvilla......................................30
Sharkey's Gold, and the Lady in the Attic......... 35
The Bloody Tree, The Jealous Phantom... 40
A Ghost in the Thomas Massey House?..............62
"Moggey"..66
Is That You, Malachi?... 69
The Aimless Apparition....................................... 74
Ghosts of the "Coast"... 79
Ghost Hunting, With a Little Help
  From My Friends... 88
Darby Ghosts..95
Mysteries of the Miller's House........................108
The Paranormal at Parastudy............................ 114
The Pink Lady... 121
Revolutionary Wraiths.......................................124
The Witch of Ridley Creek...............................129
The White Lady of Essington........................... 131
Haunted Restaurants Revisited......................... 133
Ghosts of the Greek Houses.............................. 139
The Hamanassett Haunting................................143
Colonial Ghosts... 151
Still Stalked by Ghosts?....................................156
The Nocturnal Prankster of Sweetwater Farm.. 164
And, In the End... 167
Appendix: A Ghost-Hunting Glossary.............. 171
About the Author...177

Ghost Stories of Delaware County

PREFACE
...Just so you *know that* we *know...*

"Hey, he forgot one!"

That is certain to be said after someone reads this book.

"He didn't even write about the "Ghost of Such-and-Such" or the "Haunted Watchamacallit."

It never fails to happen. Of course, this book did not include every ghost story and every haunted place in Delaware County.

The long and tedious process of searching for ghost stories never really ends. As trite as this statement may seem, there are new ghosts being created–and discovered–every day.

To my left, as I write this very preface, is a list with a dozen names and numbers and a dozen more destinations. Each name, I was told, could tell me a ghost story. Each destination, I was assured, was haunted.

There is another list that contains another dozen names. They are the names of those who

Ghost Stories of Delaware County

were contacted, but never returned calls or emails. Each of those individuals also, I had learned, would have had a ghost story to share.

But, the writer's dreaded word "deadline" loomed like a demon over my head as the publisher pressured to have this book on the bookshelves on time.

So, to my right is an empty folder. I shall transfer those names, numbers, and email addresses to that folder and label it "Delaware County Ghost Stories, Book Two."

With the additional stories and leads and contacts that are sure to follow in the wake of the release of this book, there is the very real possibility that such a book may find its way to the bookstores in the future.

Those in the ever-expanding community of self-professed paranormal researchers, ghost hunters, and aficionados of the eerie will also compare the stories in this book with the inventory of tales that have been recorded by others in other annals.

This is when the medium of a ghost book runs on a head-on collision course with an interesting but often unreliable offspring of the media.

You may remember the childhood activity, "Whisper down the alley." It was fun to realize how facts became distorted in the telling, retelling

Ghost Stories of Delaware County

and re-retelling of a story through the ears and voices of a chain of people.

When once we whispered down the alley, we now whisper on the Internet.

Call this chapter "So You Know That I Know."

Some who finish this book will recognize that several stories that have been published on various web sites have not appeared within these pages.

Similarly, more serious folklorists and historians may scoff at what they could interpret as a naive and incomplete presentation of information in this book.

This is not a history book. Every detail and fact was checked and double-checked, and every effort was made for accuracy, but this is just a *ghost story* book.

The aid and assistance of several people in the months of researching this volume cannot be praised highly enough.

I am forever appreciative of the enthusiastic, encouraging, and essential help that was provided along the way. Their names are peppered throughout these pages.

And finally, the "So You Know That I Know" feature of this book, wherein we visit a handful of web sites and search for the ghost stories of Delaware County as they have been logged on the

Ghost Stories of Delaware County

Internet, usually without attribution or any level whatsoever of investigation.

They are what I call "They Say" stories, in which an unknown "they" has somewhere in the course of time "said" that a particular place is haunted. Who the "they" is has long been obscured by time and the telling of the story. Perhaps there was a "they" somewhere, and at some time. And, perhaps what they "said" had a basis in truth.

But, the Internet has too often become a gossip garden wherein the seeds of "urban legends" have sunken their roots into the soil of reality and flimsy fallacies have blossomed as flowers of fact.

I will pass no judgement on the veracity of the following stories, and in no way do I intend to insinuate that they have no credibility or insult those who have posted them. Similarly, I, nor you, should accept the comments and claims of those who responded to the reports as the final word on the matters.

I must also add that on two of the occasions when I contacted the sites in question for elaboration, confirmation, or denial of the story, I was asked–and in one case warned–to not specify the location in a book. But, as those particular places are public places, funded by tax money, I will dare to mention them as their "stories" have already appeared on the web.

Ghost Stories of Delaware County

The first entry we shall visit is the Performing Arts Center at Upper Darby High School. The web story claims that a young man was so tormented by evil spirits there that he hanged himself. Actors and stage crew members have reported seeing the shadowy form of a hanging body backstage and have experienced myriad unexplained phenomena.

A switchboard operator at the high school assured us that the center was a separate operation from the high school and cordially shunted the call there.

A spokeswoman there admitted that she had heard the story of the suicide and the ghost, but dismissed it as "a long-standing stage crew myth."

Also in Upper Darby is the Internet listing of a ghost at St. Alice school. It is said that a man hanged himself and a former music teacher died of natural causes in the convent. He has been known to create various and sundry unsettling situations there and she has been known to have become a phantom pianist whose playing has been heard by several people there. Strange forms and startling sounds have also been reported in the auditorium, lavatories, and hallways.

An individual who said she has worked at St. Alice for some 30 years said she had never heard the stories. "It's all news to me," she said.

Ghost Stories of Delaware County

"Honestly, if that sort of thing was going on here, I think I would have heard about it."

The Williamson Free School of Mechanical Trades, near Media, supposedly hosts spirits in its George and Longstreth dormitories, and in the main building.

A spokesman there was friendly but firm in his denial of any hauntings, anywhere on the campus.

A stretch of Dog Kennel Road in Upper Providence Township has long said to have been haunted by the sobbing spirit of a young girl who died on a bridge over Crum Creek on that road. "They say" that anyone who dared to venture to that bridge at midnight would see the girl's apparition.

We took that story to Upper Providence Chief of Police Thomas J. Davis. "Sure," he said, "It's a beat-up old bypass road down at Rose Tree Park, and we've received many calls about kids 'hanging out' down there. It's spooky there at night."

Chief Davis said he hasn't heard the "girl's ghost at midnight" story as it pertains to Dog Kennel Road. "I did hear a similar story, but not on that road. I heard that a girl's body was found in Ridley Creek and her mother was so distraught that she hanged herself somewhere, along some road."

Ghost Stories of Delaware County

The chief believes the stories are typical teenage scare-'em-up tales.

The Garretford Elementary School and the adjacent convenience store are supposedly haunted by the ghosts of prisoners who were murdered by their captors and buried in unmarked graves where the school is now situated.

Two long-time staffers at the school said they have never experienced anything untoward, and had never even heard the story.

One worker at the convenience store did hear of an employee there who claimed to have seen the image of a musket-carrying, 18th century soldier glide across the parking lot and fade away as it approached the street.

Are these web whisperings and blog blurbs worthy of consideration and further investigation? Are the "theys" who "said" them out there, somewhere, and willing to say more?

That file folder to my right is a bit thin right now. It awaits any and all out there who have more tales to add to what is sure to be a growing collection of the Ghost Stories of Delaware County.

•

Ghost Stories of Delaware County

INTRODUCTION
And, an Introduction to Delaware County's own "Ghost Hunters."

Delaware County is known for many "firsts" in Pennsylvania.

The first Swedish pioneers to settle in what is now Pennsylvania made landfall in what is now Delaware County.

William Penn himself first set foot on the soil of his "sylvania" in Delaware County.

The first religious services, courts, mills, colonial assembly meetings, and untold other events and activities are among Delaware County's claims to famous firsts in the Keystone State.

Add to that the establishment of the first American Ghost Society-affiliated paranormal investigation in the Commonwealth.

"I just wanted to have an organization where people can meet and talk about the paranormal and get together to pool our interests, information, and knowledge," said Laurie Hull.

Laurie was "assigned" the coverage area of Philadelphia by the AGS, and set up shop in her

Ghost Stories of Delaware County

native Delaware County.

"I started it because there was no group in the area that investigated ghosts," she added. Laurie also became involved in the Delaware County-based Parastudy group for further metaphysical enlightenment.

"I was interested in all of this," she said, "because I grew up in a haunted house in Folsom. We all knew there was something there, and I wanted to know more."

The house, which still stands, was the home and office of a physician in the early 20th century.

"My grandmother bought it in 1965," Laurie continued. "She was very religious, so any talk of ghosts was taboo. But, ever since I was little, I didn't like the house. I felt uncomfortable there."

The house was like a second home for Laurie, as she went there every day after school. She even had her own room there.

"I stayed in my mom's room upstairs, which was the 'haunted room.' I couldn't sleep there. Often, I would be in bed and get the feeling that there was something hovering right over me. I could feel it.

"Once, my mom picked up my younger sister and took her downstairs. I was there alone, and I saw this huge, shadowy thing. It followed them downstairs."

Ghost Stories of Delaware County

Laurie believed that in addition to the "haunted room," the basement also harbored spirit energies. There was a depression in the back part of the basement floor, she noted, and added that she was convinced that it was the indication of an unmarked grave.

On one occasion, Laurie and a group of friends were gathered at the kitchen table enjoying milk and cookies. Suddenly, a strange knocking sound was heard coming from the basement. One of her friends joshed, "Maybe it's the ghost!" Laurie dismissed it nervously, "Don't joke around–it's not the ghost!" But, with that assertion, the tin of cookies flew off the table and slammed into the wall. They all looked at each other in stunned silence and left the house.

Although Laurie might have been uneasy with the notion of a ghost within the walls of her own grandmother's home, she had a quest to find out more.

Ultimately, she came to believe there were two separate spirit entities in the house–one in the "haunted room" and another in the basement.

Her own daughter once claimed to have spotted the ghost of a dark-skinned man in the basement. She said that he died there, and that his name was "Kokojam." When Laurie asked the girl how the man died, she replied, cryptically, "I think

Ghost Stories of Delaware County

he holded a gun the wrong way, and then he died."

Laurie eventually left that house and, incredibly, moved into another home in Sun Village that contained its own resident wraith.

"I was told that a former owner was hit by a car and killed just outside the house," Laurie said. "We strongly suspected that he was still there, still checking up on everybody."

Laurie and her DelCo Paranormal Research team members have investigated reports of hauntings in their own county and throughout the mid-Atlantic states. She particularly enjoys probing the ghostly energies in "public" places where skeptics or ghost-hunting enthusiasts may actually visit. And, she laments the fact that many or even most of the places the group investigates are in private houses where the property owners insist that their identities and addresses remain confidential.

Such is the bane of the paranormal investigator who "files" reports on web sites and the ghost story writer who publishes books. But, it is completely understandable.

The exchange of anonymity for credibility may make the reader uneasy and uncertain about the veracity of the report or story, allow me to assure you that no story in this book or in any books I have written has been fabricated. As once

Ghost Stories of Delaware County

said in the introduction to a legendary television crime show, "names have been changed to protect the innocent." More accurately in the case of haunted places, names have been changed or eliminated and addresses have been generalized to protect the properties and their owners.

Often, people in sensitive professional positions have experienced ghostly encounters but are hesitant or insistant that their names not be used so as to protect the trust they have earned with their clients, patients, or associates. And often, stories take place in or on properties that would be vulnerable to thrill-seeking would-be "ghost hunters" who have no respect whatsoever for the privacy of the properties or the people.

In the case files of the Delaware County Paranormal Research group, one investigation is listed as being conducted in what was only described as a "haunted barn in Delaware County."

Not only was the exact address withheld because of the privacy issue, but members of DCPR were also told that the structure was structurally unsound. They were accompanied by an individual who knew the idosycracies of the barn and what and where to avoid within its aging, failing walls.

Laurie Hull granted permission to excerpt from the group's findings when they investigated

Ghost Stories of Delaware County

reports of its hauntings on a dark night, just after midnight.

"We had been told that most of the activity that the guide experienced had occurred upstairs in the main barn area. The stairs were in bad condition, with some missing. I chose to stay downstairs with another member of the group so that we could see what developed down there. I was not getting any significant results with equipment, but the feeling of being watched was overwhelming. One of the photos taken during this time by the other member showed a misty area near the door that we entered.

"When I entered the upper level of the barn, I noticed a large pentagram painted on the floor. When I began to take some general photos, I realized that I was out of film. As I was changing the roll, I glanced up and saw the shadow form of a man standing in the doorway to the outside. I hurriedly finished loading the film, and took some pictures. One of the pictures showed a light. The second photo contained an orb anomaly.

"Of course, I wanted to investigate more closely the area where I had seen the figure. As I moved toward the area, I was overcome by a horrible lightheaded, sick, and dizzy feeling that caused me to lose my balance. I had to sit down on the floor. One of my fellow investigators came

Ghost Stories of Delaware County

over to see if I was all right, and the EMF detector jumped from a green or "safe" reading to a red "danger" reading. I got my EMF detector out and mine began to sound the danger alarm as well. The investigator helped me get up and over to the stairs. As we descended I was seized by a feeling of panic, as if someone was right behind me and wanting to push me or attack me physically.

"We continued to investigate the immediate area, and we all froze as we heard footsteps downstairs followed by a loud clanging noise as if someone were hitting a pipe with a metal object. We descended the stairs, and the noise immediately stopped. I and one member stayed by the door while the others went to investigate. No person could be found, nor could any source of the noise!

"We gathered in the stable area, and discussed possibilities. The only living things known to be there, besides us, were rats and bats! The clanging had been a regular, measured rhythm, and the footsteps definitely of two feet in shoes. As we continued to discuss the phenomena, and similar phenomena we had experienced in Gettysburg, we all fell silent again as we heard a loud thud upstairs, followed by heavy footsteps and a loud dragging sound. One member went upstairs to investigate, and I called out, 'If you want to talk, talk, but please don't re-enact

Ghost Stories of Delaware County

anyone's death!' To his great disappointment, the noise stopped as the investigator reached the top floor.

"It was getting late, so we had to call it a night at 2:30 a.m. As we walked away from the barn, we all looked back, and the feeling that someone was watching from that door was very, very strong. I went out to take a photo and my camera would not turn on. I asked another member to take a photo and his camera would not work either, so we didn't get a photo of the outside."

Laurie added that she and her associates had hoped to return to the barn in short order and search for more evidence as to its haunting.

But, the very next day after their visit, the property was cordoned off and declared off-limits.

Since then, the barn was partially demolished and what was left of it was converted into a private home.

Laurie is anxious to return to the site and ask if its new occupants have had any visits by its very *old* occupants.

Another location that shall remain nameless was a graveyard in southern Delaware County where Laurie and a friend had an eerie experience.

"The first time I visited this cemetery," she said, "it was not to look for ghosts. I wanted to look at the old headstones. As I entered the far

Ghost Stories of Delaware County

section of the cemetery, I started to feel that there was a presence there. It is hard to describe exactly what that feels like, but the closest I can come to describing it is that it is like when you walk into a room and the people stop talking. It is a slightly uncomfortable, tense feeling. At that point, I decided to return for some investigating at a later date

"I had another experience there before I could return to do any investigation. Another member and I were sitting in a car on the road next to the cemetery. It was fairly late at night, and very dark. Suddenly, I noticed a green glow coming from the cemetery. I asked the other member if he saw it, and he replied that he did. Suddenly, we were both overcome by a feeling of dread and danger, and neither one of us was able to get out of the car to investigate this phenomena more closely. We wanted to, but we were getting a clear message to stay away. We drove around the side to get a look, and we did not see anyone or anything. The glowing green spot remained stationary, and did not increase or decrease in intensity. We observed this light for about an hour, and then I went home."

Another story dear to Laurie's ghost-hunting heart is that of the so-called, elusive, "Lansdowne Ghost."

Ghost Stories of Delaware County

"I heard about this ghost when I first started seriously researching ghosts as paranormal phenomena," Laurie said.

"A former member of our group told me that the spirit of a young girl haunts the area of the intersection of Lansdowne Avenue and Providence Road in Lansdowne. The story he gave was that a girl was walking home with her bike down the hill of Providence Road coming from Lansdowne Avenue when she was struck and killed by an automobile.

"I have, since that time, heard the story from other local people, and have attempted to see this spirit for myself. Of course, the local legend is that you have to drive down the road (Providence) at midnight. Well, I can tell you that was an exercise in futility, because I have driven that road countless times at midnight and I have never seen anything unusual. I was beginning to think there was nothing to this story until the night of September 19, 1998.

"It was 10:45 pm, and I was on my way home from a friend's house. I was stopped at a red light at the intersection of Lansdowne Avenue and Baily Road going towards Providence Road, which is at the next light. This is one of those intersections with the delayed green to allow people to turn, so I was waiting for my light to

Ghost Stories of Delaware County

turn green and watching oncoming cars make their turns onto Baily Road.

"Then I noticed a woman standing in the middle of Lansdowne Avenue on the other side of the intersection, standing just on my side of the yellow line. She was facing my car, but I could not distinguish facial features. I saw the outline of her hair, which looked like a puffy '80's do, and her clothes, which also seemed very 80's. She had the acid-wash jeans, big puffy socks pulled up over the bottom of her jeans, and high top white sneakers. I was struck by the fact that she was so perfectly 80's...and she was standing in the street, arms crossed over her stomach. I started thinking, 'Oh, great! Just my luck. I want to go home, and there's some drunk standing in the road in front of my car! probably suicidal, and wants to jump in front of my car!' As I was thinking this, she vanished. It was so odd; she was there, then she wasn't there. My mind still struggles to accept what I saw, yet I know that I saw this occur.

"The next day, when I told that former member about my experience, he immediately said, "You saw the Lansdowne Ghost!!" I don't know about that. It was a block away from the traditional spot, and this image was definitely a woman, not a girl. Also, the intersection where I had that experience is at the edge of a hospital and

Ghost Stories of Delaware County

two blocks from a huge graveyard. As far as I am concerned, I still haven't seen the original Lansdowne Ghost."

Keep searching, Laurie. And, keep searching, fellow members of the Delaware County Paranormal Research group.

Remember, they are out there, those ghosts, and they shall never go away.

What's more, these ghost *stories* shall never go away. Since the dawn of recorded history, good tales of good and bad spirits have been a vibrant and vital part of our society–every society, through every age.

This book is not intended to be a history book. It is just, as the title suggests, a book of ghost stories from the then and now of Delaware County, Pennsylvania.

It is hoped, however, that this publication will take its place as a worthy companion to the history books that have been written about this most intriguing corner of the Commonwealth.

More than that, let this book be the source for tales to be told by campfire or candlelight, and a reference for those who seek to venture beyond the bounds of history.

Sleep tight tonight!

Charles J. Adams III

Ghost Stories of Delaware County

THE SNEEZING NUN
The ghost of the Mother Superior
at The Pennsylvania Institute of Technology

Does the ghost of a diminutive nun haunt the halls of the Pennsylvania Institute of Technology in Rose Valley?

There's no doubt in several of P.I.T.'s faculty and staff members that she does, and her presence has provided one of the most interesting and, in its own way, amusing incidents this writer has ever encountered in more than 25 years of investigating and chronicling ghost stories.

The Pennsylvania Institute of Technology dates to 1953 when practicing engineer Walter Garrison established it in Upper Darby. After

Ghost Stories of Delaware County

decades of steady growth, the school moved into its present 14-acre campus in 1982.

That campus had been the Notre Dame School for Girls, and there are those at P.I.T. who are convinced some vestiges of that past remain there–in ghostly form.

"There have been various sightings," said Dr. Dona Marie Fabrizio, Dean of Student Services. She continued by describing what has been seen and what most folks believe is the identity of the entity.

"She's an elderly nun, and she is usually seen in full habit. Because of the bib and the size of the hat, we assume she was the Mother Superior. It's different from the Notre Dame order.

"She's usually seen in the areas of the library, in the tower area, which is now the Garrison office area. I've been here for more than 11 years and have been told by several people that they have caught a glimpse of her."

Phenomena familiar to the follower of ghost stories have played out in the lobby and tower of the building. Doors will open and shut on their own, cold spots will be felt at certain places, things like that. "The director of admissions was down here by herself and she swears someone breezed by her," Dr. Fabrizio continued. "She could feel the cool draft on her face. It happened several times to

Ghost Stories of Delaware County

her."

The dean has also seen the ghostly nun, several times. "The last time I saw her," she noted, "we were upstairs just before the sisters' quarters were to be renovated. She was spotted at the end of the corridor. She didn't move. She didn't look angry. She just looked vigilant as if she was watching over the project."

Another individual has had a mysterious encounter with a now-you-see-her, now-you-don't kind of sighting.

Lefenus Powell is better known to his coworkers as "Bugs." A longtime custodian at P.I.T., he isn't prone to believing in ghosts, but finds it difficult to interpret a brief incident he experienced at the school.

"I was outside of the school, and it was about two o'clock in the morning," he remembered. "Just my partner and I were there, and I knew nobody else was in the building.

"I happened to look in the window and I saw an individual inside, walking past. I said to my partner, 'Hey, we have a girl walking around in there!"

Both "Bugs" and the other gentleman knew that was impossible. It was two in the morning. The building was empty.

"I'm sure it was empty," Bugs concluded,

Ghost Stories of Delaware County

"but I know what I saw. There was a woman in there, and when I tried to take a closer look at her, she just disappeared!"

Another individual, who wishes to remain nameless, substantiated what others have stated and provided his own detailed account.

"I personally saw the apparition," he said. In fact, he remembered it well. "It was roughly 10:20 p.m. on an October Thursday in 1992. I was wrapping up night class over in the engineering center and had to run up to my faculty tower office for some paperwork. I saw her just beyond the doorway leading to the old third floor board room, now Walter Garrison's room.

"It was a nun, dressed in a full habit. It looked turn-of-the-century.

"It was an extremely electrifying experience!"

It is Angela Cassetta, the school's director of administration and marketing who provided one more testimonial and the title of this chapter.

"One night we were closing up," she said. The two girls with me here in the evening were waiting for me in the hallway. I had forgotten something, so I told them I'd be right there. I ran back in my office and when I was coming back to meet them by the fireplace in the reception area, I saw her.

"She was tiny, only about five feet tall. She

was dressed in full garb. Her hands were in front of her, and she just nodded at me."

Stunned by the unexpected and unsettling vision, Angela nodded back, and remained quite calm. "The girls started screaming and freaking out," she recalled. "But, it wasn't threatening at all, it was just really cool to see her!"

That would not be the only time she would cross paths with the ghostly nun.

"It was a Wednesday, around 8:30 p.m.," she continued. "I was by myself here, and I went to the back door to lock up. My key wouldn't fit. I was struggling with the key and felt somebody right behind me. I figured it was the cleaning guy, coming over to make fun of me. Then, somebody sneezed-*ka-chew!*-on me.

"Well, I turned around, figuring it was him. It wasn't him. There wasn't anybody there, or anywhere nearby."

A bit miffed by it, Angela looked up and down the hall, and saw no one.

But again...*ka-chew!*

"Well, I said, OK, no big deal. God bless you. I calmly locked the door, and that was that."

Does she believe it was the nun–the Mother Superior–who, in ghostly form, sneezed? "Oh yes, no doubt," she said. And, she was a bit disappointed that she didn't stick around a bit.

Ghost Stories of Delaware County

"I was actually hoping to have a little more interaction with her," Angela wryly added.

•

Several architectually-significant buildings are situated on the Pennsylvania Institute of Technology campus in Media.

Ghost Stories of Delaware County

THE LADY IN BLUE

Things that went bump in the winery...

Once, there was a winery in an early 19th century barn at the end of a lane off Beaver Valley Road near Chadds Ford.

As this book was being researched, Geoff and Fran Harrington were closing the Smithbridge Cellars winery they had operated for about seven years. It was a familial, not financial decision. The winery had been good for them and good to them. But, as their families grew and aged, they realized they had to prioritize.

The Harringtons had many good times cultivating their seven-acre vineyard and producing their Chardonnay, Merlot, and Cabernet wines.

They also had a mystery in that old barn–the mystery of the "lady in blue."

"The first incident I remember," Fran said, "was in the dead of winter, in January. Somebody wanted to have an event here, and the whole tasting room was packed with people.

Ghost Stories of Delaware County

"All of a sudden, we heard this noise upstairs, as if something was being dragged across the floor up there."

The sound got everyone's attention. As they paused and tried to figure out what it might have been, Fran reckoned it was Geoff, doing some heavy-duty work on the upper level of the barn.

"Well, we were waiting, and a few minutes later Geoff came in. I asked him what he was doing up there. He said he hadn't been up there!"

Frank was incredulous. She and the others had definitely heard something–something quite loud and now quite mysterious.

"Well, we unlocked the door to the upstairs and went up there. Geoff thought that maybe something had fallen over, or maybe someone had wandered in there. We knew it couldn't be a squirrel, or anything like that. It was just too loud for that. And, the tasting room was packed and everyone heard it quite clearly."

The source of that sound remains unresolved. But, Fran did not discount the possibility that it was connected with the energies that seem to swirl within the wooden walls of the old barn.

"We had two girls helping us in the tasting room from time to time," Fran continued. "They were convinced we had a ghost in here. They would hear things."

Ghost Stories of Delaware County

One of those girls plays a role in the sighting of the "lady in blue."

"Another incident we had here was more of the apparitional variety," Fran said.

"Geoff was racking wine in the cellar and one of the girls was in the tasting room. It was just the two of them and Geoff was leaning over, working or something, and out of the corner of his eye he saw someone standing there–a female dressed in blue. He didn't give much thought to it. He figured the girl helper had come into the cellar.

"But then, a few minutes later, he went into the tasting room and saw that the girl was sitting at the counter, doodling."

Geoff had no cause for concern or a closer look when he glimpsed the blue-clad woman in the wine cellar. He had no reason to believe it was anyone other than the helper girl.

Miffed, he asked her if she had been in the cellar. She had not. And, she was not wearing blue.

Fran recalled another individual who also had a brief look at the phantom female.

"There was a couple in the tasting room with me," she said. "It was just the three of us, and I was talking to them when the lady seemed distracted. She said she saw, out of the corner of her eye, a woman dressed in blue."

Ghost Stories of Delaware County

That woman had heard nothing about any other sightings or sounds there. "But," Fran asserted, "she was convinced there was a woman in blue who appeared and then disappeared there in the room."

Who could be haunting the old barn? "Well," Fran pondered, "the farm is very old. In fact, when you come up the road to the barn, you see some ruins. That was an old cabin that burned down in the 1930s. I can only imagine all the families who lived there, and on the farm. All the love, joy, tragedies, and tears. Maybe it's someone from one of those past lives here.

"We often thought, too, that being in the Brandywine Valley, there might have been some Revolutionary War activity here. Maybe our ghost is from that time period."

No matter who, what, or when, the Harringtons and their helpers are comfortable with their spectral residents. They were never frightened by the sights and sounds. In fact, the assistants in their former winery paid homage to the ghost, or ghosts.

"It was Valentine's Day and we were giving roses to customers," Fran said. "One of the girls kidded around that we should be nice and placate our resident ghost. So, she went upstairs and placed a rose there...for the ghost."

Ghost Stories of Delaware County

The original octagonal barn at Linvilla Orchards. At the time of the writing of this book, it was being rebuilt after suffering severe fire damage

LEGENDS LIVE AT LINVILLA
Moggey's Ghost, the spirit of "Indian Hannah, and perhaps even the Jersey Devil "haunt" the landmark orchard

"In my old house that's been here for 200 years, the ghost simply moves files and papers. You put them down and they're never there when you come back for them."

The words are those of Peg Linvill, the third-generation owner of Linvilla Orchards, the landmark fruit farm, market, and attraction along

Ghost Stories of Delaware County

West Knowlton Road.

"I know there is somebody–or something–in that house," Peg continued. "It is absolutely determined to move those papers."

While the shuffling of papers is scant evidence of a haunting at the farm, there are plenty of reasons to believe that spirits do indeed roam the 300 acres of Linvilla.

The most intriguing is "Moggey."

"Moggey was a servant girl who was murdered and buried down by the ford that went across the creek at Knowlton," Peg said. "The people got spooked at night. It got so bad that they went up to the Presbyterian ford, which was much safer!"

Henry Graham Ashmead's mentioned Moggey in his comprehensive 1884 *History of Delaware County*. He cited a reference in Dr. George Smith's early (1862) history of the county:

The site of Knowlton, up to the year 1800, was a perfect wilderness. Near the head gates of the mill there was formerly the mark of a grave the occupant of which tradition named Moggey, and from that circumstance the crossing of the creek was named Moggey's Ford. As Moggey had the reputation of making her appearance occasionally, it required no little courage in the traveler in early times to cross the ford at night.

Ghost Stories of Delaware County

Old Moggey's ghost may well wander the grounds of Linvilla Orchards. At the very least, she is memorialized along the trail of the Halloween-season hayrides that course through the property.

Richard Crosby is another character whose restless, and some say quite cantankerous ghost rambles through the orchard.

One of the earliest settlers of the area, Crosby became at once a pillar and a pariah of the community.

"He was the first person to be sued in Delaware County," Peg Linvill noted.

The legal action was taken after some of Crosby's pigs wandered onto neighboring property.

Ashmead noted that incident in his history book:

In 1686, (Crosby) was presented by the grand jury "for keeping an unlawful fence to the great damage of John Martin, in his swine," for which ill-doing on his part Crosby was fined thirty shillings at the next court.

Although Crosby somehow managed to become the tax collector for what is now Middletown Township, he was quite a character. Again, from Ashmead's history:

Crosby figured considerably in the early

Ghost Stories of Delaware County

court records. *In his cups he seemed ever to run into quarrels, and if threatened with the strong arm of the law he was not chary in his remarks or the expression of his opinion of the sage bigwigs who dispensed justice in the old court house on Edgmont Street, Chester.*

These historical notes serve to suggest that as restless and offensive as he might have been in life, he may be just the same in the afterlife.

"My theory is that his ghost remains here," Peg Linvill said. And, the irrepressible Mr. Crosby is also represented as one of the subjects in the Linvilla Halloween Hayride.

Still another is Sam Riddle, a prominent man who owned land just over the hill from the orchard. Sam's noble old manor house was destroyed by a fire fairly recently.

"Sam was quite the partying type," Peg said. "Not quite what my dear father-in-law, a simple Quaker, would approve of."

He was also a noted horseman, and Peg believes his ghost, saddened after the loss of his old home, is on the loose at Linvilla–as Peg suggested, "in search of some good horse flesh!"

Peg holds the legends and lore of her area dear to her heart.

"I even have the sense that the spirit of Indian Hannah, Sandy Flash, and even the Jersey Devil

Ghost Stories of Delaware County

are here on this land," she said.

For the uninitiated, "Indian Hannah" (1730-1802) was the last of the native Lenni Lenape Indians to reside in the Brandywine Valley; and Sandy Flash was an 18th century outlaw who terrorized Chester and Delaware counties [see "Ghost Stories of Chester County and the Brandywine Valley," Exeter House Books].

As for the Jersey Devil, the beast of the Pine Barrens of New Jersey was actually sighted in Chester and Leiperville in 1909.

Real or imagined, the ghostly people and creatures that roam Linvilla Orchards are part of the history–and the mystery–of a most enchanted part of Delaware County. And, Peg Linvill has a most enchanting philosophy about it. "If you settle down and sink into where you are," she said, "you will sense these things around you."

•

THE GHOST AT "PRENDIE"

What was once an orphanage is now Archbishop Prendergast High School in Drexel Hill. And, according to local legend, it is haunted.

The ghosts of two children have materialized on the second floor, and the spirit of a nun who supposedly hanged herself in the bell tower has been heard, felt, and seen by students almost since the time the school was established in the mid-1950s.

Ghost Stories of Delaware County

SHARKEY'S GOLD, AND THE LADY IN THE ATTIC
Ghost stories from early Upper Darby

We sat at a table in a room on the upper floor of the old section of the Sellers Memorial Free Library in Upper Darby.

He spoke, I listened.

He is Thomas Roy Smith, the library archivist and the collector and dispenser of local history and legends.

The setting was perfect for the telling of ghost stories. We were in what was once called "Hoodland," the residence of Philadelphia tanner and leather processor John Sellers II.

When it was constructed in 1823, it was deep in the countryside. From its lofty position atop

Ghost Stories of Delaware County

Hoodland Hill, one could gaze across the Delaware River into New Jersey. It was known for its simple but stately architecture, and the Sellers family's substantial library.

When Sarah Sellers, the last of the Sellers family, passed away in 1933, she funded the establishment of a public library and directed it be named in honor of her parents, David and Mary.

Do ghosts haunt the Sellers Library?

"One might think so," said Thomas Roy Smith. "There are drafts, there are creaks, and other odd things happen occasionally," he said. "If anyone is to blame or credit for them, it would be John Sellers II, I suppose."

But, no substantive ghost story has sprung from the hallowed halls and walls of Hoodland.

Although Tom Smith spends the vast majority of his time researching and recording details of the times and the places, and the who/what/why/when/where of history, he did recall some stories with otherworldly overtones.

He recalled an interview with an 84-year old woman who told stories from her long life in the Addingham section of Upper Darby.

Most were random familial memories, but one spanned several generations and, perhaps, the perceived limitations of life itself.

"She told me that she happened to go up into

Ghost Stories of Delaware County

the attic of her family home," Tom said, "and up there was a trunk. Now, she had been up there before, of course, but that particular time, she was startled by something.

"She said she saw a woman, dressed all in white, with long, gray hair. She was just sitting there, on the trunk, motionless. She couldn't believe her eyes!"

She went back downstairs to the kitchen, where family members had gathered. "She told everybody what she had seen," Tom said.

As she described the mysterious woman she had seen in the attic, it became clear to the elders that she was describing a former resident of the house. It was a woman who owned that trunk, and it was long known in the family that the trunk contained the woman's trousseau and other personal belongings–her hope chest–and it was just left in the house when the property was sold.

"She had been afraid that some relatives in Clifton Heights would get hold of the items after her death. It was her dying wish that the trunk remain in the house. As it turned out, after she died, her relatives couldn't have cared less about its contents. So, it went up the stairs and into the attic."

Even as an octogenarian, the woman insisted she had not fabricated the story, and was

Ghost Stories of Delaware County

convinced that she had seen the form of the woman, sitting on the trunk, jealously guarding it for eternity.

As a serious folklorist, Tom Smith has a theory about certain kinds of stories that survive the telling and retelling of them through the years.

He refers to them as "folk explanations."

"I believe that, for example, when I ask how a place got its unusual name, there is probably an innocent suggestion with only a shred of truth. But, all of a sudden, it takes on a life of its own as factuality."

He is also fascinated how stories transmute in the telling.

An example is the tale of "Sharkey's Gold."

Some call it the "Garrettford Gold," as it was in that section of the township where the story played out in the late 19th century.

Daniel Sharkey and his wife were tenant farmers in western Drexel Hill. "Mrs. Sharkey was looking over the field out back, and at the base of a chestnut tree she noticed a hole that had apparently just recently opened up. She reached in and discovered gold...lots of gold coins!"

Interestingly, Tom Smith has discovered two versions of the story. "When it was told by a man, it was *Mr.* Sharkey who discovered the gold cache. When women told it, it was the *Mrs.* who found it.

Ghost Stories of Delaware County

So, is the "Sharkey's Gold" story mere legend?

"What might have been the source of the story is that these people were quite poor, working as dirt farmers, and all of a sudden they were wealthy," Tom theorized. "That, then, is a solid 'folk explanation.'"

But, there may be a baseline to the story in the annals of hard history.

"Supposedly," Tom added, "a Colonial soldier in the Revolutionary War era had a premonition that he would be involved in a battle and was carrying on his person a good sum of gold.

"He was passing through the area and stashed the gold in the crotch of the tree for safekeeping while he was off to war. When he returned, he would retrieve the gold.

"But, he never returned. His premonition came true and he was killed in battle. And, that's how the gold remained there up until the time that Mr.–or Mrs.–Sharkey discovered it."

•

THE CHESTER SCHOOL DEMON

A schoolhouse that once stood at Fifth and Welsh Sts. in Chester was said to be haunted by a so-called "Caco-Demon" (in tradition, the most evil demon of all). The story was the talk of late-19th century Chester.

Ghost Stories of Delaware County

THE BLOODY TREE, THE JEALOUS PHANTOM...

...and other ghost stories from Delaware County's dark past

When it comes to a good, old-fashioned ghost story, times haven't changed all that much in the last two centuries.

Relating to ghost stories told to him in his youth, a noted Delaware County historian and writer noted:

The localities where these incidents of the past were laid, necessarily became places of dread, and oftentimes when in the dusk of the evening, I, or any in the locality where these stories were said to have happened, we felt the awe of our surroundings. I remember my heart beats would be audible to my own ears, and I would quicken my steps until finally I would break into a run, looking constantly back over my shoulders, in fear that some frightful shape was in pursuit of me.

The writer was Henry Graham Ashmead, and the words were from a paper presented to the Delaware County Historical Society in 1902.

Ghost Stories of Delaware County

The following serves as a solid bridge between the stories told by an heir to Ashmead, Thomas Roy Smith and a modern-day investigator of haunted places, whom we shall meet in the next chapter.

•

In my early boyhood days, on winter evenings when the winds would whistle without and make strange noises in the chimney, I have often listened to the stories of supernatural occurrences and ghostly visitations.
–Ashmead, 1902

Although some locations given have long been obliterated by houses, highways, commercial and industrial developments, the challenge for the contemporary ghost hunter is in pinpointing them with the scant information given.

One of the stories collected by Ashmead was that of a tree that wept blood.

The time was on an autumn day in the early 1700s, and the setting was somewhere along the King's Highway in Lower Chichester, near Trainer.

A well-dressed young man was found bludgeoned to death at the foot of a small tree. His head had been bashed in, and blood soaked the trunk of the tree. Brain matter and ripped bits of flesh saturated the ground.

Ghost Stories of Delaware County

The crime baffled the crude local constabulary. The victim was never identified, and the killer was never brought to justice.

It was said that the following spring, when the leaves of that tree sprouted, they were of a deep, crimson color–the color of blood!

What's more, when a curious passerby took a closer look and snapped a twig from a branch of the tree, it drained a blood-red sap.

Superstitious folks were convinced that the tree had been somehow infused with the lifeblood of the murdered man, and nature–or a higher force–had ensured that his brutal death would be perpetuated in its fearful foliage.

The "Bloody Tree" was supposedly cut down and its roots were burned by a later property owner who had grown tired of curious ghouls who gathered there.

•

Out on the Edgmont great road, near the Middletown Township line, it was related that often the ghost of Genase Burgess had been seen by belated persons who traveled that highway after midnight and before the cock's crow in the morning.

–Ashmead, 1902

A classic case of a jealous lover sets the stage for this story. But, there is a ghostly twist, of

Ghost Stories of Delaware County

course.

Genase Burgess was well up in years when he married a much younger, beautiful woman. One would think the May/December marriage would have served to make Mr. Burgess a very content man in his last years.

But, he was obsessed with the fear that her love for him was not eternal. It worried him until the day he died. And, even after his death, he wanted her to be his and only his. He made a pact with himself that would surely shame the young woman into never marrying again.

It is recorded that in his will, read in November, 1767, he included a provision that his body be buried under the pavement that led to the front door of his house. That way, he believed, his widow would have to pass over his mouldering corpse each time she departed and returned. It would, he was certain, keep her faithful to his memory.

But alas, it was not to be!

For whatever reason, Burgess was buried in the garden of the property, far from the front walkway. If he had hoped that his burial at the threshold of his home would have prevented his widow from marrying again, those hopes were dashed when she took a new husband shortly after his death.

Ghost Stories of Delaware County

It was believed by neighbors that the ghost of the betrayed Genase Burgess rose from his misplaced grave and prowled angrily throughout the house and garden. Wherever that property once stood, and whatever is there right now, his energies are still likely to ramble.

The next story from Ashmead's eerie archives might be easier to pinpoint.

•

When I was a small lad, we boys were loath to be caught at nightfall in the neighborhood of that dwelling and when in wagons, would urge the horses to almost a run until we had passed out of ear-shot and all danger from uncanny influences had been left behind us.

–Ashmead, 1902

That neighborhood was described as "on the Telford road, on the north side of the highway in Leiperville, with the B&O siding along the west side of the house."

And, it was the lair of the ghost of Jeremiah McIlvain.

The circumstances of his death were tragic. Jeremiah had apparently committed suicide by plunging down into the deep well on his property. His son, Spencer, was distressed when his father was missing for several days. Suspecting the worst, he had friends lower him into the well,

Ghost Stories of Delaware County

where he found his father's bloated corpse.

The forlorn spirit of Jeremiah was said to be imprisoned forever on that land.

•

Who she was, where she came from, or what was the motive for the act, was never learned, but often it was said, on stormy nights by the uncertain glare of vivid flashes of lightning, a woman's figure would be seen in the archway.

–Ashmead, 1902

The archway in question was at an old granary at Second and Edgmont Streets. A rough-and-tumble section of town, it was there that the badly-battered, bloody body of a young and lovely woman was discovered in an archway that led to the riverfront docks.

Although neither her nor her killer's identities were ever ascertained, she "lived on" as a well-known and often-seen ghost in that archway.

Then–and perhaps still today–her spirit rises as a misty figure with arms cast skyward.

•

Luke Nethermark was a young man residing near Muckinipattas Creek in Lower Darby Township.

–Ashmead, 1902

And, it is Luke Nethermark who rides forever

Ghost Stories of Delaware County

in that region on his spectral steed.

Luke had been visiting friends and had been enjoying a day of conviviality and camaraderie. As evening approached, threatening black clouds gathered and thunder rumbled in the distance. A storm was on its way, and Luke had to be on his way, as well.

His friends advised him, and then implored him to stay and wait out the storm until it passed. He was even welcome to stay overnight, if need be.

But, Luke was determined to ride home, and believed he could do so before the storm reached its peak.

The clouds thickened, the thunder quickened, and lightning flashed all around him. Still, he urged his horse through the gathering gloom. He reached the White Horse Level when it was clear he would not escape the savagery of the tempest.

As he whipped his horse to a gallop, rain pelted him and darkness wrapped around him like a cloak.

At once, his trusted horse was tripped by the trunk of a large tree that had been felled by lightning only seconds before.

The horse tumbled violently, breaking its own neck and back. Luke Nethermark was thrown from the saddle to the ground, and his mortally-

Ghost Stories of Delaware County

wounded horse came crashing down on him, crushing him to death.

Many people, so long ago, reported seeing the ghostly horse and rider speeding along the Chester Pike. They would appear at any time, but in the thick of a thunderstorm, they would be seen actually reenacting the horrible fall that led to their deaths.

The Prospect Park Historical Society has placed the optimum site for a Luke Nethermark sighting as the old White Horse Tavern, at 705 Chester Pike.

A published account puts the tragic incident there, and in 1756.

And, it is there that at least one other ghost is believed to dwell. It is the spirit of a Captain Culin, of Ridley, who was shot to death in front of the tavern by a soldier who was angered after being reprimanded by him.

•

The story is threadbare by frequent telling.
—Ashmead, 1902

That is the fate of many a good, old ghost story, and challenge to the collectors of same.

Details become warped and distorted as the tale is whispered down the alley of time. Names, places, and time frames become muddy and muddled.

Ghost Stories of Delaware County

In the nearly three decades that I have been researching and writing ghost stories, I have marveled at how some of the stories I published a generation ago have come back to me in a form I hardly recognize.

In the tradition of the great Irish writer W.B. Yeats, who collected "threadbare" tales of banshees, faeries, and ghosts in his native land at the end of the 19th century, H.G. Ashmead did much the same in Delaware County.

One of them was yet another horse-and-rider phantom tandem.

But, the events that were the baseline of this particular ghost story proved to be more chilling, perhaps, than the ghost story itself.

It is filled with tragedy and intrigue and fraught with confusion, misinterpretation, and misinformation. It is a story of sex, morality, murder, political intrigue, a wrongful execution, an undelivered pardon, ghosts, and a hermit.

It has all the elements of a Hollywood movie.

We turn back the pages of time to the time of the Revolutionary War, when sentiments of farmers and townsfolk in Delaware County were sometimes split between allegiance to the Crown and the efforts of those who sought independence.

Elizabeth Wilson was the daughter of a farmer who was a staunch Tory. When the British

Ghost Stories of Delaware County

captured Philadelphia in 1777, she took it upon herself to spend several weeks there. And, it was there and then that she met a handsome army officer.

Elizabeth had stayed in the city with family friends, but later sought to secure a job and more permanent residency.

She found employment at a tavern where, conveniently, her soldier friend was a boarder.

No doubt, she dreamed of a future as the wife of the dashing soldier and the mother of their children.

That dream would never come true. In fact, she could never have imagined what horrors would confront her.

For years, the two carried on a torrid affair, but the young man never asked for Elizabeth's hand in marriage. One day, Elizabeth came to the realization that she was pregnant, and despite her pleas, the child's father refused to marry her.

Elizabeth was scorned and scandalized. She was asked to leave the house in which she resided. Her young life was falling into a funnel of misfortune.

Despondent and desperate, Elizabeth sought comfort and understanding in the only refuge she knew, on her father's farm and in her father's arms.

Ghost Stories of Delaware County

But, she was a shamed, disgraced woman. Even the bonds of father and daughter were not strong enough for her to present herself to him as her daughter in her time of need. Instead, she approached her childhood home cloaked and clandestinely. It is said that when her father heard the knocking on the door and asked who was there, she replied, "a poor, sick woman."

Incredibly, her father did not recognize his own daughter. His second wife, Elizabeth's stepmother, hadn't known her at all, and upon realizing the girl was pregnant, assumed all matronly duties.

Not long after giving birth to two boys, Elizabeth was on her way back to Philadelphia to find their father.

What happened in the ensuing weeks would only come to light in the closing moments of what was left of Elizabeth's sad life.

What is known is that she eventually returned to the inn in which she had worked. Old friends said she appeared disheveled and disoriented. No man accompanied her, and while they knew she was pregnant when she left, she had no baby or babies with her when she sought sanctuary at the inn.

At just about the same time, a group of hunters made a grim discovery in the woods near

Ghost Stories of Delaware County

what is now Edgmont Avenue and Providence Road. In a shallow, common grave at the base of a tree were the battered bodies of two newborn boys.

As primitive as the forensic techniques might have been, it didn't take long for authorities to reckon that the infants were those of Elizabeth Wilson and the unknown father.

Elizabeth was taken into custody and charged with the murder of her babies. Before Judge William A. Atlee, she offered no plea of guilt or innocence, sobbed hysterically, and begged for mercy. She was moved swiftly though the judicial system and no defense testimony was presented. With nothing more than circumstantial evidence to ponder, the jury deliberated for hours and, before a hushed courtroom gallery, delivered a guilty verdict. Judge Atlee, bound by the procedure of the day, immediately sentenced Elizabeth Wilson to be hanged on the gallows in Chester on December 7, 1785.

Having been spurned by her friends and even abandoned by her own father, the doomed young woman would die alone and forsaken.

Somehow, her brother William, who had been living and working on a farm in Lancaster County, learned of Elizabeth's plight. He was determined to console her in the last days of her life.

In a visit arranged by local clergymen,

Ghost Stories of Delaware County

William went to Elizabeth's side in the county jail. Elizabeth was overcome with comfort and joy. Her spirit and hopes lifted, she pleaded with her brother to listen to her side of the story. He said he would do so only if there were witnesses to whatever she had to say.

He convinced Judge Atlee, the county sheriff, the prosecutor and the public defender to join him in Elizabeth's cell. It was only days before the scheduled execution.

Having been counseled by pastors and having regained her senses, Elizabeth was clear and collected as she spoke.

She told them that in those weeks during which her whereabouts were unknown, she had actually arranged a rendezvous with the father of her twin boys. They had met in the woods, and she dearly hoped he would accept them as his children and her as his wife.

He would have none of it. He showed no compassion, no mercy. He refused to accept that he was the father of the children, accused her as a sinner and them as bastard children.

Incredibly, he demanded that Elizabeth destroy the babies. She shrieked and wept at the thought. She ordered him to go, and take his callous thoughts with him. With that, he drew a pistol and again insisted that she kill the boys–or

Ghost Stories of Delaware County

he would.

In an uncontrollable fit of fear and shock, Elizabeth refused. The boys' father then took the babies from her arms and flung them to the ground. As he held the gun to her head, he crushed the life out of the boys with his boots. He threatened her with death if she ever told anyone about the unthinkable deed.

Gripped by grief and fear, Elizabeth endured the following weeks as a broken woman. When accused of the murder of her children, she remained mute.

Her jail cell revelation took the breath away from all who listened. The judge, sheriff and attorneys were so convinced that she was telling the truth that they drew up a document that would offer a stay of execution, but only if it was certified by the Executive Council in Philadelphia.

That assignment was accepted readily by William Wilson, who embarked immediately on a quest for justice.

He had only days to accomplish the heroic and, quite possibly, quixotic feat. It was the dead of winter. The weather was horrible. The Schuylkill River was strewn with massive chunks of ice and was flooding. He was becoming increasingly ill and his horse was becoming increasingly weak.

Ghost Stories of Delaware County

Still, William Wilson persisted. Through the darkness of night and a driving rainstorm, he managed to make it to the capital and the Executive Council.

Now, with only hours before his sister was destined to die in "Hangman's Lot" near the spot where her babies' bodies were found, a weary William faced knee-deep mud on the roads. Emboldened by the life-sparing document he clutched in his vest, he plodded on.

In Chester, Elizabeth was being prepared for her execution. The judge, sheriff, and lawyers were truly hoping, and the clergymen were praying that William would make it to the gallows in time to present the pardon. In fact, the sheriff sent deputies along the Queen's Highway and had them positioned at critical turns. If and when they would spot William Wilson, they would flutter large white flags progressively down the line toward the gallows as a signal that the reprieve was on its way.

Still, the authorities were bound by the law. Slowly and methodically, the sheriff led the condemned woman onto a cart that would carry her to the noose.

All eyes were on the white flags carried by the deputies up the road. Those gathered to witness the execution were morbidly silent. As time ticked down to the predetermined and legally-bound moment of death, no white flag waved.

As the rope was knotted around her neck, Elizabeth was given the opportunity for a final statement. She assured all that the account she gave in her cell was true and prayed for her soul, and the souls of her slain babies.

It was reported that few of those gathered at Hangman's Lot actually saw Elizabeth Wilson drop from the horse cart and die. Their attention was turned instead to the white flags that extended up the roadway.

Too late!

Still, the thud of the rope stiffening, the snapping of the neck and the gagging sound of the girl's death throes were unmistakable. Elizabeth Wilson was dead.

Ghost Stories of Delaware County

The crowd stood in stunned silence. A full 15 minutes or so went by as the woman's body was removed from the rope and placed in a simple pine coffin.

Those solemn, quiet moments were shattered as a flutter of a white flag was noticed and the beating of a horse's hooves was heard in the distance. Soon, the words *"A reprieve!...A reprieve!"* echoed in the woods.

William Wilson had arrived with his sister's stay of execution. But, he was too late–23 minutes too late.

Seeing his sister's body and reeling from his tortuous journey, William collapsed in sheer exhaustion.

He was taken in by folks in Chester and given a place to rest and recuperate from his noble but, ultimately, futile mission.

For several weeks, he suffered with a fever and hallucinations. Eventually, he recovered enough to return to his home in Lancaster County.

But, in one final twist to the story, William Wilson chose to not return to that home, or to any shred of civilization.

Visitors to Indian Echo Caverns, near Hummelstown, Pennsylvania, will hear the story of "The Pennsylvania Hermit."

He lived a solitary life inside the cave for

Ghost Stories of Delaware County

nearly 20 years, sustaining himself by making millstones and selling them to local millers. He rarely strayed from the cave, and spent much of his time reading the bible and writing.

The "Pennsylvania Hermit" was William Wilson.

William Wilson, The Pennsylvania Hermit
(Illustration from "The Sweets of Solitude")

Ghost Stories of Delaware County

In addition to the legend he became, Wilson also left a legacy in the form of a twelve-page essay that extolled the solitary lifestyle and adherence to Christian principles. His *The Sweets of Solitude, or Instructions to Mankind How They May Be Happy in a Miserable World* was retrieved from his meager belongings and published after his death. The only known original copy of it is in the Free Library of Philadelphia, but the entire text is available on several internet web sites.

William Wilson died in October, 1821, and his obituary in the *Harrisburg Intelligencer* encapsulated his tragic tale:

His retirement was principally occasioned by the melancholy manner of the death of his sister, by which his reason was partially affected. She had been condemned to die near Philadelphia for murder, in the hope of concealing her shame from the world, and the day of execution was appointed. In the mean time her brother used his utmost means to obtain her pardon from the Governor.

He had succeeded, and his horse foamed and bled as he spurred him homeward. But an unpropitious rain had swollen the stream, he was compelled to pace the bank with bursting brain and gaze upon the rushing waters that threatened to blast his only hope.

Ghost Stories of Delaware County

At the earliest moment that a ford was practicable he dashed through, and arrived at the place of execution just in time to see the last struggle of his sister. This was the fatal blow.

He retired to the hills of Dauphin County, where he employed himself in making grindstones for a livelihood.

One morning he was found dead by a few of his neighbors, who had left him the evening previously in good health."

In the passage of time, and perhaps in an attempt to distance himself from his sister's woeful life and death or seek a more profound anonymity, William Wilson may have played a trick to confuse and confound whomever might have taken an interest in his writings. The author of *The Sweets of Solitude* was credited as "Amos" Wilson. And, in the introduction to the essay, his sister's name was given as "Harriot." Historical researchers, however, have no doubt that the document was written by William Wilson.

The Elizabeth Wilson matter has spawned a number of ghostly legends, from just days after the murder of the children to the present day.

In very early accounts, it was said that the sad sound of newborn babies wailing could be heard in the woods where Elizabeth's boys were murdered.

And, nearby, on the Hangman's Lot, or more

Ghost Stories of Delaware County

recently Gallows Hill, the ethereal image of a woman has been seen wandering. Witnesses say her head is bowed and she wears a cream-colored, long dress on her gloomy glide through eternity.

For several years, several people who worked in a restaurant at the approximate site of the old gallows reported many totally unexplainable events inside the establishment. One woman, who asked that her name not be used, described the old Howard Johnson's restaurant as "very haunted, by very weird happenings."

She said items would disappear and reappear on a regular basis, and she and others would see filmy forms of individuals float past the counter and in the parking lot.

"One of the girls was convinced that she was in communications with the spirit of a young girl there," the former waitress added. "She told me the girl was sad because she had killed her children."

Then, the waitress could only shrug at her co-worker's claims. But, when she was informed about the location of the gallows and the sad tale of Elizabeth Wilson, she was staggered.

"Unbelievable! That waitress who told me her story is gone now, but now, finally, maybe I can believe that she wasn't making it all up!"

Who knows, perhaps even today, in that criss-

Ghost Stories of Delaware County

cross of roads where the gallows once stood, or in the present-day diner, nearby hotel, or any of the other buildings on Gallows Hill, the spirit of Elizabeth Wilson, or any of the others who met the hangman there may still roam. And, when conditions are right along Providence Road, the ghosts of William Wilson and his horse may still be seen and heard on their frantic ride. The dull roar of a horse's hooves, the crack of a whip or reins, and the misty blur of the man and beast may materialize as they replay the ride over and over, forever.

•

THE GHOST OF A "BATTLE-AXE"

In 1840, Aaron T. Morton plunged a razor into his throat, slashed it from ear to ear, and died a bloody death on his farm in Ridley Park. It was a grisly end to a life that had been tormented by the teachings of Theophilus Gates, leader of a bizarre cult known as the "Battle-Axes." (See the strange story of this group in "Ghost Stories of Chester County and the Brandywine Valley," Exeter House Books)

Morton was driven to kill himself by demons that swirled in his mind, and did so in dramatic fashion, to the shock of a group of neighbors.

It has long been believed that Morton's ghost, blood streaming from its neck, can still be seen on the site of his old farm. That farm was on land that is now consumed by the Taylor Hospital.

Ghost Stories of Delaware County

A GHOST IN THE THOMAS MASSEY HOUSE?

Does a Colonial soldier stand eternal guard at one of the most historic houses in Delaware County?

One can only imagine the Delaware County landscape when the first Europeans built their settlements on its rolling hills and fertile soil.

Sadly, little remains of those earliest endeavors, but here and there are shreds and shards of the past.

One of them is the Thomas Massey House in Marple Township. It is one of the most important structures not only in the county, but in the entire

Ghost Stories of Delaware County

Commonwealth.

Thomas Massey set foot on this soil in 1683 and was among the first English Quakers to settle in Marple Township.

He was not a rich landowner or nobleman. He was a 20-year old indentured servant who worked for a landlord until the terms of his servitude were satisfied.

Massey was diligent, and earned 100 acres to call his own. He married Phebe Taylor and they raised seven children on a "plantation" that would eventually grow to 300 acres.

The house was expanded and modified over the centuries, and the last Massey family member sold it to outside interests in 1925.

By 1964, it faced a date with the wrecker's ball. A descendant of Thomas Massey, Lawrence M.C. Smith, came to the rescue when he purchased the house and one acre around it and transferred the deed to the township.

In the following decade or so, the township restored the house, documented its historical and architectural significance, and opened it for visitation.

Those who come to call these days will find a period garden that is cultivated in season, living history demonstrations, and guided tours.

And, they might find a ghost that some say

Ghost Stories of Delaware County

strolls through the house and grounds.

"Quite a few years ago," said Rich Paul, vice-president of the Thomas Massey House, "two women were here, and one of them looked to the other with a shocked expression on her face. She said she saw a Revolutionary War soldier in the house!"

There were no reenactors there that day, and nobody dressed in period garb. The woman was convinced that she had seen the ghost of a Colonial soldier.

Paul's own daughter, who is sensitive to ghostly energies, once visited the house and astounded her father when she looked at him and said, point-blank, "There's somebody here who is not happy!"

Paul asked his daughter what she meant.

"She told me she had the sense that there was a male entity there who was not happy. He wants to know why you call it the Thomas Massey House!"

Rich Paul had no answer, other than the obvious one–that it was, well, Thomas Massey's house.

He's on the fence as to his own thoughts about a ghost roaming the historic property. But, he did offer a thought.

Rich Paul found it curious that one of the

Ghost Stories of Delaware County

spirits believed to be in the house was that of a soldier, as Thomas Massey was a Quaker, and the house was a place of peace.

But, research has revealed that one former resident of the house, Joshua Lawrence, did serve in the Revolutionary War. Lawrence was actually born in the house. "Maybe he's the ghost," Paul said. "And, maybe he thinks the place should be named after him!"

Thinking a bit more, Paul quipped, "Well, it *is* on Lawrence Road. But, I guess that's not enough for him."

•

"WE HEAR THINGS..."

The Delaware County County Historical Society purchased the circa-1830 "Greenbank Farm" on Palmers Mill Road in 2001. The Society is phasing in various operations at the property, with the "Passport to History" offices being the first to move in.

Passport coordinator Gayle Foulge was asked if there has been any ghostly activity in the fieldstone farmhouse.

"We hear things," she said, "and we've experienced things here that are not quite normal. Maybe they are paranormal. We'll find doors open that we know had not been open. And, our resident cat all of a sudden gets spooked and runs across the room for no apparant reason.

Some there have traced the possible haunting to a drowning they believe occured in a pool that once adjoined the house.

Ghost Stories of Delaware County

"MOGGEY"
The Ghost of the Ford

We met Moggey briefly earlier in this book as a character represented during the Halloween season at Linvilla Orchards.

We met H.G. Ashmead earlier in a chapter dedicated to his remembrances of early legends and ghost stories in Delaware County.

We now bring Miss Moggey and Mr. Ashmead together and examine more closely what is certainly among the most enduring legends of rural Delaware County.

Just who Moggey was, whether Moggey was her first or last name, and why she came to be buried in a solitary grave between the mills along the Chester Creek at the Knowlton Road ford were all mysteries by the time Ashmead recorded the tale in his definitive history of the county in 1884.

Ashmead himself referred to an earlier county history published by Dr. George Smith in 1862: "Near the head gates of the mill," Dr. Smith wrote, "there was the mark of a grave the occupant of which tradition named Moggey, and from that

Ghost Stories of Delaware County

circumstance the crossing of the creek was named Moggey's Ford. As Moggey had the reputation of making her appearance occasionally, it required no little courage in the traveler in early times to cross the ford at night."

Ashmead was fascinated by the stories he had read and heard.

"Why the woman had been interred there or why her uneasy spirit lingered about that place is not known in all its details," he wrote.

Even the form and fate of the phantom of the ford were matters for discussion by the scholarly types who dissected the legend.

"The traditions associated with that grave took many forms," Ashmead noted. "A woman betrayed had drowned herself to escape the blight that had fallen upon her life; a husband in a paroxysm of jealousy had slain his wife and buried her by the ford, years after on his deathbed disclosing the crime for which he had never been tried; unrequited love had driven a heartsick girl to the rash act..." All of these versions of the victim's fate were offered.

Ashmead also pointed out that the ghost of the young woman took on divergent appearances.

"As a boy I had heard aged people assert that they had known in their youth persons who solemnly declared that when driving across the

Ghost Stories of Delaware County

ford at night they had seen the shadowy outlines of a woman's figure standing by the lonely grave, her unsubstanial body, which refused to rest in the tomb, offering no impediment to the star beams, which, passing through her form, glistened in the stream as if nothing had impeded their course.

"That could not have happened if the woman had not been a phantom–a reminder of a bloody deed unavenged by justice."

Is Moggey a myth, only a legend of long ago?

What I like about retrieving these types of stories and presenting them to a new generation is what I believe intrigues you who read them.

Neither writer nor reader know, and neither Dr. Smith nor Mr. Ashmead knew much more about Moggey, and even the precise location of her haunting.

Therein is embedded the very essence of a good ghost story–mystery.

Find that creek crossing, that "Moggey's Ford." Visit it on a star-strewn evening. Linger quietly until a dim glow rises from the soil and is silhouetted in the darkness. Whisper her name in the night...*Moggey...Moggey...is that you, Moggey?*

Will she answer? Probably not.

But then again.....

•

Ghost Stories of Delaware County

IS THAT YOU, MALACHI?
Disenchanted spirit roams Springfield's historic Lamb Tavern

If you're looking for good food served in a wonderful atmosphere inside an historic structure, you will find it at the Lamb Tavern on West Springfield Road in Springfield.

If you're looking for a ghost, you may find one there, too.

Tavern owner Steven Graham kindly gave us a tour of the "non-public" areas on the upper floors of the building and admitted that he had

Ghost Stories of Delaware County

never sensed any spirit activity in the place. "This is not to say," he said, "that there's not something here."

He confessed that he felt and respected a sense of history that permeates the establishment, and invited us to see what we could see and sense what we could sense in the search for ghosts there.

What we found is strong evidence of ghostly energies there and what could well be an equally strong baseline for any haunting there.

The "we" in this case includes the author and a "sensitive" individual who wishes to remain anonymous. "Frankly," she said, "I'm a teacher in a district in Delaware County and I wouldn't want some people knowing what I do in the paranormal field." Let us, for reference only, call her "Molly."

According to a history provided by Mr. Graham, the Lamb Tavern has stood at its present site since 1808, when it was known as the "Three Tuns." It was named the Lamb in 1835.

While it has been operated by a long line of innkeepers, it is one, who owned it in the late 19th century, who may hold the key to the haunting.

According to the historical timeline, a strange and tangled chain of events and innkeepers extended from 1866 to 1881.

Simply put, when one of the proprietors

Ghost Stories of Delaware County

named Malachi Sloan died in 1881, a provision of the innkeeper's last will and testament stated that the Lamb Tavern would never again be operated as a hotel. The reason for that demand was never quite clear.

What is clear is that the Lamb Tavern is a "hotel" of a sort for at least one eternal guest.

As Molly and I settled in at a table at the restaurant, she switched into her "ghost hunting" mode. No electronic equipment was necessary, no theatrics were needed. Only what Molly jokingly calls her "receptors" were employed in this most informal of investigative styles.

She did not enter into a trance, did not lapse into a mystical netherworld. She simply observed and absorbed the energies that swirled around her. Those seated at table around us would never have known what was happening. And, oh yes, it should be noted that no liquid spirits figured in our meal, just water and diet soda.

"What a marvelous place," Molly said as she looked around the dining room. "I can feel the history, and, yes, there seems to be a presence here."

Molly has a good track record. "It's not as if 'I see dead people,'" she quipped, "it's just that I get feelings and bits and pieces of evidence that somehow add up to something being there, on another level."

Molly prefers to enter an alleged "haunted" place with no predisposition, no knowledge of who might haunt it and why. Such was the arrangement at the Lamb Tavern. Of course, she knew why she was there–to "read" the building. But, she knew nothing of its history. What's more, as its current owner mentioned, there had been no substantive stories of ghosts there.

That would all change as Molly revealed her findings.

"First, I believe it's a masculine spirit, a man," she said. "And, he seems bewildered, confused, as if he has some sort of unfinished business here. He means no harm, and, because 'he' is just energy, can do no harm.

"I think, though, that he is disenchanted, if that's the word."

As she further interpreted her psychic feelings, something quite interesting started to come into focus.

"I can almost sense a name, or names," she added. "The name 'Mallory' or 'Mordecai' or 'Mal-something' seems to come to the forefront."

Uh, Molly, could that be "Malachi?" As in the Malachi Sloan, whose will contained that odd inclusion?

"Well," she responded after I asked her that

Ghost Stories of Delaware County

question, "you're not going to believe this, but as I was trying to nail down a name, Malachi came to mind. For whatever reason, I didn't say it."

As she continued to unravel her revelations, she said the energy seemed the strongest toward a doorway that leads into the barroom area of the building and at a door that leads to the upper floors.

"I sense that the spirit, in life, was very protective of the inn, and is basically that way still today. His energy is a warm energy, if you know what I mean, but on another level it seems as if the man's personality is at once protective and perplexed. I have a feeling, and it's just my interpretation of this, but I have a feeling that someone did him wrong here one time, in a business deal or something, and that's why his energy was deposited or imprinted here."

Did Malachi, or the spirit that Molly detected, die in the Lamb Tavern?

"That, I'm not sure about," she said. "That would be a question for historians or genealogists. All I know is what I feel, and it's just the feeling that the energy, or the *ghost* of a man, whose name could be Malachi, seems to be here, has been here for a long time, and will remain here forever."

•

Ghost Stories of Delaware County

THE AIMLESS APPARITION
The sightings of a suicide victim at the Pace One restaurant

Tucked in a glen in Thornbury Township is a village where the pace of life in Delaware County seems to slow down a bit.

As suburbia creeps up all around it, the crossroads hamlet of Thornton remains quaint and quiet. There's a post office there (which, some believe, is the oldest in continuous use in the country); a sturdy old home (once the summer home of George Gray, the operator of the 18th century Schuylkill River ferry and namesake of the Philadelphia neighborhood); and a handsome stone barn with its own pace–namely, Ted Pace.

Ted is the owner of the Pace One restaurant, which is situated inside the ca. 1740 fieldstone

Ghost Stories of Delaware County

barn. He holds dearly the history of that little corner of Delaware County, and finds fascination in the mystery of his own nook of that corner.

That mystery has apparently spawned a ghost story at Pace One, and Ted Pace believes he can trace the origin of it.

"It goes back to the early twentieth century," he said. "There was a man who lived here who was sort of a freelance waiter for the 'landed gentry' around the region. We don't know much about him.

"We *do* know, though, that he ultimately hanged himself from a beam on the third floor of this building, when it was a barn."

That unfortunate and unidentified chap may still be, pardon the pun, "hanging around."

Ted lives on the fourth floor of the former barn. "I personally have experienced nothing," he admitted. "But, I think I've heard enough stories from others that there has to be something to it."

He invited us to speak to any of his current or former staffers who might have had brushes with the mystery phantom there.

We needed go no farther than Gloria Walker Burger, who worked at Pace One for ten years and crossed paths with the ghost there on several occasions.

"I had never had an experience before," she

Ghost Stories of Delaware County

said. "Actually, I saw him for several months before I said anything to anybody. I was new there and didn't want anyone to think I was weird."

The sightings of the spirit remain vivid in Gloria's memory.

"I would always see a man. He was dressed in dark clothes, a long jacket, and sort of baggy trousers. He didn't have a lot of hair, maybe he was bald.

"When I first saw him, he would just walk in front of me, and I would actually talk to him. I would say, 'hey, could you grab that salad and take it to table four,' or something like that.

"He would walk right in front of me, but I never did see him straight on. I always saw him in the corner of my eye, just off center. He was clear, but always just off to my left or right."

Gloria described him as a short man, and as she said, she held the matter close to her vest for awhile. To her surprise, however, another waitress volunteered to her that *she* had seen the figure of a man inside the restaurant. The two compared notes.

"We started to discuss what we saw and we both saw the exact same thing in the exact same places."

What perplexed Gloria the most is that the man would often favor what she called "dead-end"

Ghost Stories of Delaware County

rooms.

"I would see him go into the coat room, or the liquor closet and just disappear," she recalled. "And, the only time I saw him upstairs, it was the clearest vision I ever had.

"I saw someone go into an empty dining room. Now, it's easy to get lost in Pace One, so I followed him into the room and said, 'Excuse me, sir, can I help you?' Well, of course, when I walked in, there was nobody there and there was no place for anybody to go!"

Gloria remembered other staff managers who may never have seen the ghost, but who have been impacted by its energies.

A manager was closing the restaurant for the night, and had gone through all the motions of doing so. Lights out, stoves and equipment off, etc., etc. She went into the office to shut down the computers and worked her way back outside, through the kitchen. To her astonishment, every burner in the kitchen was on!

"She did not want to stay there late by herself anymore," Gloria said.

Another employee was closing on another night, and after going through all the motions inside, she locked up and went to her car in the parking lot. She was distracted, looked back at the barn and saw that every light was lit! Luckily, a

Ghost Stories of Delaware County

waiter was still in the parking lot and he accompanied her back into the building and turned off the lights.

Those occurrences could not, of course, be directly linked with the energy of the man who killed himself in the barn. But, that energy may be so intense that it could affect the building's electrical, plumbing, and piping infrastructure. Such phenomena are not unusual in cases of hauntings, and especially where a suicide is involved.

So, was Gloria ever frightened when she saw the aimless wraith of the restaurant?

"No," she said. "I never thought it was a scary thing. My friend who saw him also didn't feel it was a menacing presence.

"We talked about him, and we came to the conclusion that it was probably the man who killed himself on the third floor and he was having trouble finding his way. It's as if he's lost, or something, and just wandering around the restaurant."

•

Ghost Stories of Delaware County

GHOSTS OF THE "COAST"
Tales of pirates, ghosts, treasures...and trash

The menacing chap in the drawing above is none other than Blackbeard, the legendary pirate. And no, never shall it be claimed that the

Ghost Stories of Delaware County

ghost of Blackbeard haunts Delaware County; and never shall it be claimed that any of his treasure is buried here.

But, if only in legend, Blackbeard has left his mark on what has been called "Pennsylvania's Southeastern Coast."

The river towns of Delaware County have always been ports of importance and intrigue.

The first tale to rise from the ripples of the river was the 1716 account of a ship's captain who was carried away by the devil himself just off Marcus Hook.

The story was recorded by a Rev. Andrew Hesselius, who swore it was a true story, not a preacher's parable.

"The captain of a ship, well-known in Pennsylvania, on his way home from the West India Islands, was suddenly carried out of the ship, in sight of all the people on the ship, upon whom he vainly called for help."

The captain was described as a callous, wicked man who had deceived members of his crew and duped women in every port of call.

"No doubt," Rev. Hesselius speculated, "he had a secret pact with the devil."

As his vessel was anchored in the river, the ship's captain had a sense that his transgressions had come back to sting him. "He had himself

Ghost Stories of Delaware County

bound firmly in his cabin with a strong rope and warned all of his approaching doom," the minister said.

The pilot approached the manic master with a bible and attempted to read from it and fend off the demons that had gathered. "But," the story continued, "the bible was violently snatched out of his hands and thrown to the ship's mast."

With that, the captain himself was ripped from his bindings and hurled into the water.

"All the people were almost crazed with horror and some of them had to be kept in fetters of iron lest they should lay violent hands upon themselves," wrote Rev. Hesselius.

The ultimate fate of the captain was never revealed in the story, but it's a fair bet that a bit of repentance may have shaken him to his senses.

While that tale is not a ghost story, *per se*, the next account is a classic.

The suggested viewing point for the ghost may well be the vicinity of Gov. Printz State Park in Essington. Although the precise location and date of the incident has been washed away in time, it has been recorded as taking place at an area that seems to be in that vicinity.

In his "Early Clergy of Pennsylvania and Delaware," published in Philadelphia in 1890, Rev. S.F. Hotchkin wrote:

Ghost Stories of Delaware County

"There was a tradition extant among the country people that a boat's crew from the British fleet, then in the river, landed at the beach and proceeded inland to plunder the inhabitants.

"Before their return some of the country people came down and shot the boat keeper. In my early day, the story was current that the ghost of the dead sentry could often by seen at midnight walking up and down the sandy beach between the big trees.

"Children avoided going there after dark."

The story was more than a childhood chiller, according to Delaware County historian H.G. Ashmead, who mentioned with his customary flair a reference to the sentinel's ghost by U.S. District Attorney Aubrey H. Smith.

"When he was a boy, he had talked to several elderly persons who firmly declared that they had seen the spectral marine years before, who scoffed at the suggestion that their imaginations had deceived them and that an impression of the mind had appeared to them in the garb of reality."

Ashmead said he was told the event took place on a clear, moonlit night in early autumn, 1777. He described the spirit's nocturnal perambulation:

"The place where the marine fell had become haunted ground, and for years afterward it was asserted by residents of the locality that on the

Ghost Stories of Delaware County

night of the anniversary of his death, a spectral British marine in the uniform of that day, could be seen walking his post, his figure, on occasions when the moon was full, being magnified in the hazy light. And yet, those who saw the apparition declared no shadow accompanied the ghostly appearance as it paced its fatal beat."

But what about the buccaneer whose fierce face graces the first page of this chapter?

Could Blackbeard the Pirate have really visited Delaware County, Pennsylvania?

He certainly could have, and for a reason that has brought sailors to shore for centuries–a woman.

Again, we turn to the dusty history books, and the 1857 tome, "Watson's Annals of Philadelphia and Pennsylvania," by John F. Watson.

"There is a traditional story," he wrote, "that Blackbeard and his crew used to visit and revel at Marcus Hook at the house of a Swedish woman, whom he was accustomed to call Marcus, as an abbreviation of Margaret."

There is ample evidence that Blackbeard (a.k.a. Edward Teach or Edward Drummond) sailed up the Delaware Bay and River, and some believe he was prompted to do so by his first mate, Israel Hands, a native of Cape May, New Jersey.

Blackbeard's exploits on the Pennsylvania

Ghost Stories of Delaware County

"coast" come into clear focus in the eyes of Michael Manerchia in Marcus Hook.

Manerchia owns what is called "Blackbeard's Mistress's House" on Market Street.

It is reputed to be the house where the aforementioned "Margaret" resided and provided rest and relaxation for the pirate. Whatever else she provided for Blackbeard is a matter of titillating speculation.

The Pennsylvania Historical and Museum Commission has declared the building eligible for the National Register of Historic Places, and has placed its construction date as circa-1683.

Mike Manerchia has been told privately by state officials that it could well be among the most historically significant structures in Pennsylvania, due to its antiquity and architecture. Its alleged connection with Blackbeard doesn't diminish its importance, either.

At the time of the the publication of this book, however, Manerchia was facing the daunting task of fending off the plunderers not of the sea, but of the land.

"My wife and I bought it to downsize," he said. "When we started to renovate it, we found that the original house was still intact. But, for some reason, the town wants the house torn down for a housing development.

Ghost Stories of Delaware County

Determined to do all he can to prevent that, Manerchia has hosted a parade of archaeologists, architects, historians, and preservationists and has formed a nonprofit organization to raise awareness and funds for the restoration of the house and open it as an educational resource.

Should that happen, those who tour or visit Blackbeard's Mistress's House might be wise to look over their shoulder every once in a while for the ghost that Manerchia believes dwells within the planks and logs of the building.

"It's no joke," he asserted. "We actually discovered the presence in a picture."

"I had uncovered a fireplace in the main room that had been bricked up. I was pointing out the crane hook in the fireplace and my sister snapped a picture. Over the top of my forearm appeared the face of a man with an eye patch! it was kind of a skeleton face."

Seeing is believing, and there is no doubt that the "face" is there, glaring down at Manerchia. If it is merely an illusion created by the pattern of bricks, mortar, and light, it is a truly *remarkable* illusion.

In his unbridled campaign to save the house, Manerchia has developed an intimate relationship with the place. He is also firmly convinced there is spectral activity there.

Ghost Stories of Delaware County

"We would be at the house in the summertime, when it was around 90 degrees outside," he remembered, "and I would go in the house and I could see my breath, it was so cold in there at spots!"

He dismissed it as a quirk of an old log cabin, but knew the temperature variation was far beyond the norm. "And then, we saw those pictures," he quipped.

As he removes and catalogs the artifacts that continue to emerge from behind walls and under planks, he is finding no 17th or 18th century treasures, but some trash of the era. "It's unbelievable what we have found in there," he said.

Manerchia has also found a hidden door that he believes led to an addition to the dwelling. It was in that demolished section that a clergyman may have been vexed by an unwanted spirit.

"One of the ghost stories goes back to the time when a minister lived there," he said. "Every time he would leave the house to preach, he would return to find the house in disarray. He got so mad that he had that section of the house torn down."

"I love the place," Mike said, "but I will not stay there after dark by myself anymore!"

•

Ghost Stories of Delaware County

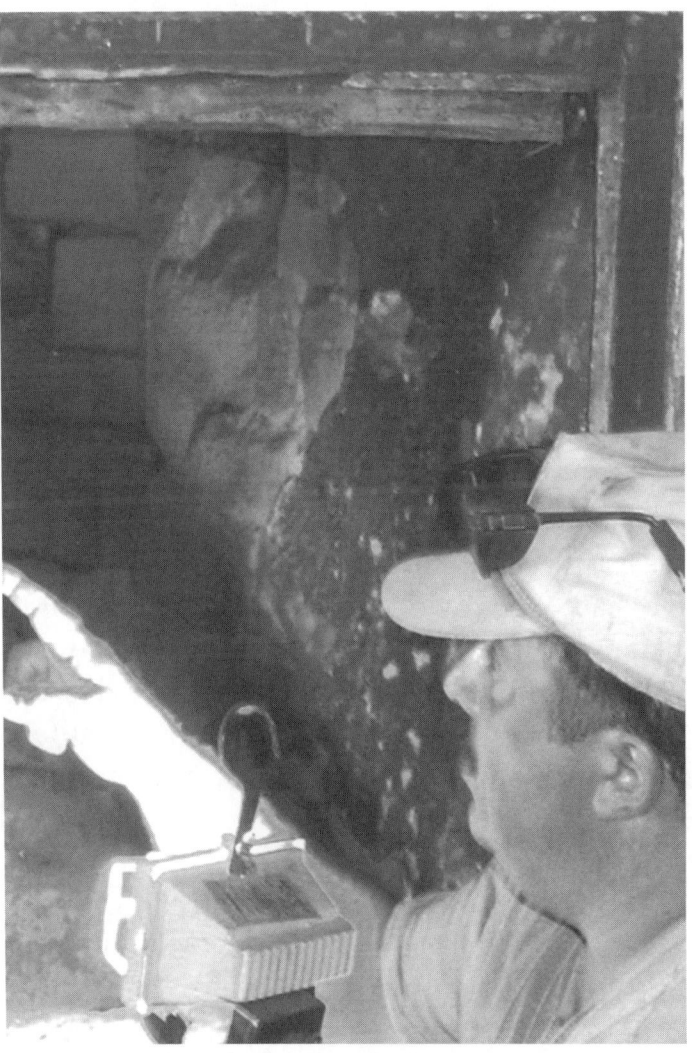

Is this the image of a ghost peering down at Mike Manerchia? The owner of Blackbeard's Mistress's House in Marcus Hook believes it is, and that it proves there is both mystery and history in the ancient house. (Photo courtesy of Mike Manerchia, Used with permission)

Ghost Stories of Delaware County

GHOST HUNTING ....WITH A LITTLE HELP FROM MY FRIENDS...

Ghost story "magnet" shares tales

One of the joys of researching a book about haunted places is meeting fascinating people who have had their own experiences or can point to others who have had brushes with the unknown.

In the course of gathering tales for this book, we met Jen O'Hare, who has had a lifelong interest in spirit activity and has become a veritable magnet of ghost stories told to her by friends and acquaintances.

Ms. O'Hare was excited about the prospect of a book about Delaware County ghosts, and offered to secure leads and names of those who had told her of their experiences over the years. She went beyond the bounds of expectation and made my job much easier by tracking down and relating the stories. What you are about to read are her words.

Ghost Stories of Delaware County

As the stories are "second hand," and as the names and addresses of those who provided them have been changed to protect their privacy, there may be the reluctance on the part of the reader to believe them. But, Jen assured me that every one is true, as told to her by people she trusted completely. They are the account from ordinary Delaware Countians with most extraordinary stories.

"The first one is from a friend of mine. I'll call her Shelly. It starts out in a big house in East Lansdowne. The house is approximately 100 years old.

"Shelly's older sister had a full length mirror in her bedroom. All three sisters had slept in the room one time or another. All three had experienced a ghostly form looking at them through the mirror. No one said a word about this until they were in their teens.

"When they shared their stories, it turned out that they all had seen the same thing. It appeared to be an old man in a full length trench coat, old top hat and he was about 5'10" tall.

"Shelly and her younger sister came home one day to find the bar stools were spinning out of control. Both girls didn't bother to investigate because they were the only ones home and they knew what was doing it. They ran out of the house

Ghost Stories of Delaware County

and waited until someone else got home.

"Her oldest brother had an encounter with the ghost when he was in his early twenties. He was sleeping in his room when he was awakened by a tapping on his shoulder. When he rolled over to see who it was he saw the old man leaning over him. When her brother realized what he was seeing, the ghostly figure stood up and walked across the room and out the door.

"A couple of times in the middle of the night Shelly's parents would be awakened to the sound of paper rustling down stairs. When they would go down they would find newspaper thrown all over the floor as if someone was looking for something.

Shelly's parents still live in the house today. They believe the ghost may be a previous owner. It was said that the man was working on his roof when he slipped and fell to his death."

Jen's second story came from a woman who lives around the corner from "Shelly," and is a good friend of hers.

"Doors rattle, footsteps, sounds of tapping on the windows and furniture moving are all some of the things this family has had happen to them while they lived in the house.

"For a long time the sounds mainly were sounds of squeaking or tapping on windows. But one night she and her sister had the scare of a

Ghost Stories of Delaware County

lifetime.

"They were in bed when they heard what sounded like furniture moving in the attic. Both knowing there was none up there, they got a little frightened. Then they heard footsteps coming down the attic steps. With that the door knob started to rattle. The footsteps started down the hallway towards their bedroom. The windows in the hall started to shake as the footsteps got closer. The girls were frozen with fear when their bedroom door knob started to shake.

"Now, being young girls in a Catholic school, they had Rosary beads in their room. The beads happened to be hanging on the door knob when suddenly there was a loud shaking noise as if the door was about to explode.

"All of a sudden the noise got so loud and the Rosary beads flew off the door knob and burst all over the floor. The girls were screaming by this time when their parents came running in their room. As their parents came in the sounds suddenly stopped. They said everything went real still.

"Everyone in the house has had something happen to them. Some have heard the sounds of someone running right by them, down the steps and out the front door. Others have heard whispers and others have seen things moving. No one

Ghost Stories of Delaware County

knows who or what this ghost may be but they are certain someone or something is definitely there."

"Another story comes from a friend of mine. Her family doesn't want to be mentioned either.

"I can tell you they live in Upper Darby. They have never seen a ghost yet, but they know there is one there. They have come home to find every drawer and door possible in the kitchen open. If something couldn't be found they would always find it later sitting on a table in one of the rooms on the first floor.

"They finally got to the point were they would start asking the ghost to find whatever it was they were looking for and it would be there later. Numerous times they have seen utensils move across the table and fall to the floor. This has happened many times. Although things don't happen all the time, it has happened enough for them to believe that someone else is still living in their house with them."

"My last story is a friend of ours who lives with a ghost on a property near Newtown Square. He lives in what used to be a barn of some sort. The main house is is quite old and the barn is a little newer. The barn was rebuilt due to a fire. The mansion is more 150 years old and the barn is around 125 years old. He has lived there for about three years.

Ghost Stories of Delaware County

"Things were quiet for about the first three weeks when he moved in. After that all hell broke loose. He was in the living room when he heard the sounds of pebbles or marbles being thrown down the steps. When he got up to look there was nothing there but he could still hear the sounds going down the steps.

"After a few minutes it stopped. Things were quiet for awhile until he came home from work one day to find his light fixture on the floor. The light was not broken, which from the height of the ceiling it should have shattered into a thousand pieces. When he looked up in the ceiling he said the wires were hot and there was a lot of paper stuffed up in the ceiling. He said it was as if someone was trying to warn him that it could have caused a fire.

"A couple of times he has had a few dates there and the ghost did not like it at all. The ghost, which he thinks is a woman, would start making all kinds of noises. She would start throwing things down the steps, or the door, which was bolted shut, would start opening and slamming shut. A couple of times a friend of his which happened to be a girl, would go over to visit and there would be the sound of banging on the walls. Another time he saw her in the middle of the night going through the kitchen. A woman even saw the

Ghost Stories of Delaware County

ghost looking out of his window.

"Mike, which is what I'll call him, said he has been awakened by her numerous times. He says he tells her to stop and that he is trying to sleep and then all is quiet. He has only seen her a few times but he almost always feels her presence. One time he actually got physical with her. Mike was bending down painting some baseboards when the phone rang. He said he got up to answer it when he ran right into her. He said he could feel himself hitting her. He started to say he was sorry when he realized what had just happened.

"Mike seems to think he knows what his ghost's name is but, for the privacy of the property owners I can't tell you that. He said he kept asking over and over again what her name was. After a few nights of this he woke up to hear someone whispering in his ear. She was telling him her name.

"The ghost seems to be very protective of Mike. The only time she won't make a fuss when a woman is in the house is when it is his mom or his sister. She sounds a little jealous to me!"

•

Ghost Stories of Delaware County

DARBY GHOSTS

A haunted graveyard, tunnel, and rock are among the borough's ghostly sites

The notion of hunting for hauntings conjures up classic "dark and stormy night" scenarios where the ghost hunter prowls at midnight through the corridors of a creepy house or between the tombstones in a ghoulish graveyard.

But, ghosts do not have clocks. They do not check their watches, discover it's midnight, and head out for a night of haunting. The energies of the departed are out there, everywhere, every hour of the day and night.

Indeed, it was not a dark and stormy night at all, but a bright and delightful day in Darby as I went in search of haunted places there equipped with some of the best aides a ghost hunter could ever ask for.

With me was a guide who is very interested in the pursuit of the paranormal, the town's premiere historian, and a lifelong resident who is passionate about her home town and who just happened to serve on borough council.

The history of Darby is fascinating, and some of the individuals and events in that history have

Ghost Stories of Delaware County

left indelible marks in legend, lore, and ghost stories.

Scrape off the stucco, aluminum siding, and false facades of many buildings in Darby, and it's easy to imagine the town in its glory days. Look above the first-floor level of storefronts and magnificent examples of architecture still remain.

We turned our car around in a vacant lot where the Arlington Hotel once stood. "It was either here, or just up the street on another vacant lot where the Buttonwood Hotel once stood, that W.C. Fields was born," said Lindy Wardell, president of the Darby Borough Historical and Preservation Society.

"His parents worked at several hotels," she continued, and it's not clear in which his mother gave birth."

It is known for certain, however, that the legendary comedian (real name, William Claude Dukenfield) was born *somewhere* in Darby, and the fact that it's a mystery as to exactly where is itself the stuff of legend.

Another legend related to the Darby kid everyone called "Whitey" is that his epitaph on his tombstone reads "On the Whole, I'd Rather Be in Philadelphia." Actually, there is no tombstone (he's buried in a columbarium niche) and it says no such thing (it simply reads "W.C. Fields 1880-

Ghost Stories of Delaware County

1946").

This tale of one of Darby's favorite sons was one of many local legends that rolled from the mind and memory of Lindy Wardell as we drove the streets of the town.

Our first stop was Boone's (or, sometimes spelled Boon's) Tunnel, a dark, dank cavern that carries Pine Street over Amtrak rails in the heart of town.

Named after one of the earliest landowners in what is now the borough, the tunnel has somehow been nicknamed by some locals as the "Mummy's Tunnel."

The bizarre moniker harkens to long-held beliefs that ghostly energies swirl within its vaulted brick confines.

"I know that it's been called haunted," Lindy said. "People feel that there are ghosts here. They feel that there is something about one woman who is said to have died in the tunnel that keeps her spirit within it."

Carol Grosso-Sollenberger, a Springfield resident who has had a lifelong interest in the paranormal, also cited a fatal train/auto collision that might have been the baseline for the haunting.

The third member of our expedition into the underbelly of history in Darby was Helen R. Thomas, who was running for mayor at the

Ghost Stories of Delaware County

BOONE'S TUNNEL: A note that should be obvious: Although the tunnel is easily accessible, it is certainly not advised that would-be ghost-hunters enter it. It is private property, and the tracks within it carry active Amtrak trains.

Ghost Stories of Delaware County

time this book was being written.

"There are all kinds of stories," Helen noted. "Any one of those that involved a death in here might have contributed to the rumors that is haunted."

Our next stop was another landmark of legends.

It is actually in the borough of Colwyn, tucked along Cobbs Creek adjacent to Darby.

As we passed the Colwyn School, Helen recalled a ghostly legend there. But, we were headed for a massive, split boulder known by some simply as "The Big Rock" and in history as "Anne's Rock."

It had been some time since Lindy and Helen had been to the rock. But, just beyond a borough recreation and swim area–and again on private property–we found it.

The rock is a geologic marvel, an Ice Age relic that has been the subject of post card views and the setting for picnics in the past. But, it now stands on what has become hardscrabble land and is far off the beaten path.

One section of the rock towers perhaps 25 feet above the ground several yards from Cobbs Creek. The other section, separated from the larger portion by a pathway, looms over the creek.

Exactly who "Anne" was remains a mystery.

Ghost Stories of Delaware County

It is believed that the ghost of a young woman named Anne haunts the massive boulder in Colwyn that bears her name.

Lindy Wardell has heard two versions of the story. One involves an Indian maiden who leaped from the rock into the creek after a breakup with her one true love.

Or, was Anne actually a Catholic nun who, in relatively recent years, committed suicide there? That version seemed to be more believable and more likely, in both Lindy Wardell and Helen Thomas's thoughts. Be it either the Indian or the nun, the stories of the haunting there have persisted for generations.

Ghost Stories of Delaware County

Ghosts are said to roam the rugged terrain of the Darby Friends Burial Ground. The site is treasured by historians, but has been trashed by vandals. Among those interred there is John Bartram, the "Father of American Botany" and namesake of Bartram's Garden in Philadelphia.

Ghost Stories of Delaware County

Next on our tour of haunted sites in Darby was the Darby Friends Burial Ground.

It stands not far from a cluster of historic properties that includes the Darby Library (the oldest continuously-operated library in the nation), the Fearne Mansion, and the Darby Friends Meeting House.

This heart of "old Darby" was a crossroads of commerce, the seat of an important Quaker congregation, and it was on a "main line" of the Underground Railroad. It beats with untold tales of intrigue, mystery, and ghosts. And, it throbs with *told* tales, as well.

As we rambled up Main Street, Lindy and Helen shared many remembrances of the neighborhood. When we reached 1205 Main, we pulled into the parking lot next to one of Darby's most endearing and endangered buildings.

"I remember coming here a lot," Helen said. "Many years ago, I helped clean this place up. Myself, my husband, and friends helped clean it when we were about 19 or 20 years old."

Today, the historic Bunting House/Friendship Freedom House is forlorn but not forgotten. Concerned citizens in Darby are determined to restore it.

Built between 1699 and 1723, the house is one of a handful of buildings that still stand on the

Ghost Stories of Delaware County

property of the landowner John Blunston. His descendants, the Bunting family, owned it until the mid-20th century.

"It was very active during the years of the Underground Railroad," said Helen Thomas.

"And," added Lindy Wardell, "there is supposedly a ghost inside."

It is the ghost, she said, of a baby whose cries have been heard by former tenants in the building.

As we walked from the Bunting House to our next stop, both Lindy and Helen lamented the condition of the house, the overgrown gardens, and the adjacent vacant properties.

Their sorrow spilled over to the entrance of that next stop, the Darby Friends Burial Ground.

"This was the walk of tears," Lindy said as we ascended the fairly steep hill that led from the tumbled-down gates to the top of the burial ground hill.

She was referring to the era when the deceased were carried from the Meeting House to their graves. But, the walk into the cemetery today is equally sad for those who cherish history.

The rugged, rutted walkway is strewn with litter. The stone steps and walls are broken, and what is standing has been desecrated by graffiti-scrawling vandals. The tall stump of a dead tree towers over the entrance.

Ghost Stories of Delaware County

Rows of weatherworn grave markers, most no bigger than a shoebox, are embedded into the soil, but many have been rendered totally illegible by time and tempest.

Still, the burial ground seems to cling stubbornly to whatever dignity remains there.

Laurie Hull, director of the Delaware County Paranormal Research group, visited the graveyard on a ghost-hunting excursion:

"The broken beer bottles and various other debris scattered around this cemetery are evidence of its current esteem," she stated in her report.

"The overall feeling is one of sadness and neglect," she continued.

She took several photographs in the graveyard, but no "orbs" or anomalies showed up. Laurie did, however, pick up an EVP (see glossary) that piqued her curiosity.

"It sounds like the voice of a woman and she seems to respond to what I am saying:

"Me: Wait till I get my digital camera!"

"Woman's Voice: Time to go home?"

"This is an approximation or interpretation of what I hear on the tape as far as her response. She sees to have an unusual accent, but the words sound like English."

There have been other reports of ghosts gliding through the graveyard. One anonymous

Ghost Stories of Delaware County

account claimed that the shadowy form of a uniformed man was seen roaming between the tombstones near the back edge of the burial ground. While the type of uniform wasn't quite clear, the witness believed it may have been of the Civil War era.

Another individual who lives in the neighborhood approached me when I returned to the graveyard with a "sensitive" individual who was anxious to visit the burial ground.

"You goin' up there?" she asked as I turned into the walkway that led to the cemetery entrance. When I replied in the affirmative, she warned me that it was a "nasty place."

By that, I figured she was referring to the broken bottles, brambles, and rugged terrain.

"There's ghosts up there," she exclaimed with all sincerity.

"Oh yeah?" I countered.

"Yeah, I seen one of 'em," she replied.

Of course, my interest was tweaked. She lingered only long enough to tell me about one encounter that assured her she'd never go back there again.

She said she was "hanging" with two friends there (not causing trouble or vandalism, she assured me) when she felt that some invisible force had come between them. She said the others didn't react, but she definitely believed that what she described as a "ice cold puff of air that just stood there" mingled with them.

She said she knew right away it was a ghost. She had heard stories that the place was haunted, but never believed in ghosts. "I didn't believe, and I couldn't have cared less about spooks," she said. "But I know that what came up to me that day, up in that graveyard. It was a ghost!"

She said she was fixed on the feeling and amazed that her friends didn't react. She became detached and backed away from them.

"That's when I saw it," she said, her words trailing away with nervous sincerity. "Right where I felt the coldness, I saw, for just a couple of seconds, an old woman."

The street-smart attitude she displayed when she approached me had quickly mellowed into respectful retrospection.

"I just stayed in my own little world for a few minutes," she continued. "I know what I saw. It was an old woman, I could tell by the dress. I think she had a hat on, because I can't remember her hair or anything. I don't know if she was white or black, or young or old. It all happened real fast. It was, like, it just showed up to let me know she was there. It disappeared real quick. That's really all I can tell you."

Ghost Stories of Delaware County

I asked her if she really believes she saw a ghost.

"I do," she said, with conviction.

I asked her if she now believes that ghosts exist.

"I do," she nodded.

I asked her if she wanted to go up into the graveyard with me.

"I *do not*," she said, in no uncertain terms.

My companion that day had already made her way through the burial ground as I was talking to the neighborhood girl.

She made her way down the hill and offered her conclusions.

"It's a sad, sad place," she said. "And, I'm not talking about its condition. I feel there are multiple presences there, some very restless and others somewhat content but quite morose. It's an overall sense of foreboding up there. I'd have to spend more time there to try to single out one or two spirits, if indeed I could."

I posed one simple but vital question to her:

"Is this, then, what you would call a 'haunted cemetery,' as some have called it?"

"Of that," she said with confidence, "there is no doubt!"

•

Ghost Stories of Delaware County

MYSTERIES OF THE MILLER'S HOUSE
A ghost finds peace at the Newlin Mill

The Newlin Mill and its adjacent park is an oasis of pure country in the ever-encroaching suburbia that surrounds it.

Situated along the Baltimore Pike at South Cheyney Road, the park is easily missed in the whirl of traffic that passes by it every second of the day.

Ghost Stories of Delaware County

The history of the mill is part of its charm. Another part is the structural and natural preservation done there by the Nicholas Newlin Foundation, a nonprofit organization created in 1957 by a ninth-generation descendant of Newlin, who received the original land grand from William Penn in 1685.

The grist mill was built in 1704 by Nathaniel Newlin and the surviving structure is one of the oldest of its kind in Pennsylvania.

The mill, and the adjacent miller's residence, are both full furnished and open for tours. There are other buildings on the site, a picnic grove, recreational fields, a fishing pond, and three miles of hiking trails.

It is in the miller's house, built in 1739 by Nathaniel Newlin III that a family living there had a series of inexplicable experience that led them to believe there was a ghost on the property.

The incident was detailed in Elizabeth P. Hoffman's 1992 book, *In Search of Ghosts*.

And, it is remembered well by Blanche Biegenwald, who has been a member of the Chester Heights-based Parastudy, Inc., for more than 40 years.

Blanche, who also serves on the group's board of directors and publishes its *Parastudy Review* newsletter, agreed to share information she

Ghost Stories of Delaware County

gathered when she and other members of Parastudy were told the tales of the haunting of the miller's house by those who experienced them.

It was 1963, before the park had been developed, and the family—we shall call them the Whites—were renting the miller's house. Mrs. White—we shall call her Claudia—was a member of Parastudy, and came to the organization with a laundry list of untoward episodes in their ancient abode.

"She had had a number of encounters with a ghostly female form in her home from time to time," Biegenwald wrote in the *Parastudy Review*.

"She was never quite sure if she had been picking up a strand of the past's vibrations via psychometry or whether she was actually interacting with a ghost. Claudia was psychically sensitive, that much we know."

Mrs. White described the spirit as "dressed in somber clothes, with her hair tightly pulled into a bun." Her appearance led Claudia to believe she could have been a Quaker.

Although the apparition was never threatening, it did cause some concern.

"On one occasion," Biegenwald continued, "Claudia saw her pull out a drawer in the kitchen, and root through its contents, as though diligently searching for something. When Claudia spoke to

Ghost Stories of Delaware County

her, she vanished, but the drawer remained open!"

The ghost was spotted about a dozen times in various rooms of the house. On one occasion, Claudia witnessed the figure sobbing on the front porch.

As Claudia dealt with the sightings, she invited other members of Parastudy to make psychic readings of the miller's house. Various levels of intensity and information were detected by the sensitives who came to call. Tales of violent deaths, tragic accidents, and agonizing illnesses emerged from the building's past.

Throughout the initial phases of Claudia's sightings and sensings of spirit activity, her husband–let us call him Bob–had written them off as a product of her "overactive imagination."

But, his attitude changed when the entity made itself evident to him.

"One day," Blanche Biegenwald continued, "as Claudia and Bob returned home in their car, the ghost was pacing across the porch. She was dressed as Claudia had described. The figure looked directly at them in the car and quietly vanished. This time, they both saw her! Bob ardently searched the premises, but found nothing. He was incredulous but, analyze it as he would, he found the episode impossible to deny."

The Whites' son also claimed to have seen the

Ghost Stories of Delaware County

spirit on the third floor bathroom of the house.

In her recapitulation of the events that took place in the early 1960s, Blanche Biegenwald valiantly and professionally attempted to sort out the details of a series of seances that were conducted in the miller's house in an attempt to identify the ghost, and interpret the circumstances that *made* it a ghost.

Those details have been largely lost in time, but according to what Blanche could patch together, a team consisting of a parapsychologist, a trance medium, and several sensitives "read" the house and conjured up its eternal resident.

While the Whites' feelings were that the ghost was gentle, the medium was "inhabited" by a most vindictive and vile Civil War-era female with issues regarding her son. The proceedings of the seance were dramatic, but wracked with inconsistencies and unconfirmable details.

"It seems that, after 40-plus years, fact has become folklore, and I have one 'cold case' to research! It *is* a Parastudy story, as virtually everyone involved had some connection with Parastudy."

But, the Parastudy group has a very "hot case" in its very midst, as we shall discover in the next chapter.

•

Ghost Stories of Delaware County

In addition to the female spirit detected in the miller's house at Newlin Mill, the ghost of a "burly man" wearing a leather apron was spotted in the mill itself by a former tenant on the property. The entity was further described as wearing 18th century-style work clothing and was dusted from head to toe with flour.

Ghost Stories of Delaware County

THE PARANORMAL AT PARASTUDY
Spirits don't stand a ghost of a chance going unnoticed at one Delaware County location

Ghost Stories of Delaware County

There is one place in Delaware County that any ghost is highly unlikely to remain unsensed or unseen.

It is the charming Victorian home of the venerable group called "Parastudy, Inc."

Long before self-proclaimed "ghost hunters" banded together in search of the unknown, Parastudy was pioneering the quest for spiritual and parapsychological understanding and personal growth.

It all started in the mid-1950s as a study group that centered on the psychic readings of Zoe Nickerson, and was formed as the Brookside Study Center in Brookside, Delaware. In 1959, a nonprofit organization was founded and established its headquarters in the handsome Valleybrook Road, Chester Heights house the following year.

Members and guests gather there for lectures, workshops, discussions, and the "unrestricted search for enlightenment."

Topics of talks and classes have ranged from wicca to reiki, meditation to metaphysical development, and a wide variety of topics in between–and beyond.

As Blanche Biegenwald noted in an article that appeared the *Parastudy Review*, "Parastudy's lovely old Victorian house is perhaps too well maintained to look the part of the stereotypical haunted house, but over the years, strange things have happened there to a number of our members and visitors."

When Blanche looked inward for the article about the ghosts of Parastudy, she found an astounding array of accounts from a broad spectrum of eyewitnesses.

"We've had many ghosts that have manifested one way or the other," she said. "That's understandable because of our collective interests. As people would pass on, they would realize that here is a place they can go where people can see them!"

There seems to be nary a nook nor cranny of the house that is untouched by the (usually) unseen.

Several members and others who have "read" the place believe there may well have been an unfortunate event that led to the untimely death of a child in the house, long before Parastudy occupied it. Others, including Blanche, believe the spectral activity there is the result of "energy patterns" deposited by the dramas and traumas of many people who lived, loved, and perhaps died in the building over the years.

As those who gather at Parastudy are the cast and crew of the *living*, the house itself is a

Ghost Stories of Delaware County

veritable theme park of hauntings.

Several years ago, the Parastudy people were told that ghosts had been reported in the building before they occupied it.

In 1982, descendants of the Voigt family, which owned the property before Parastudy, visited.

By that time, members and visitors' accounts of ghostly goings-on were legion. They felt an obligation to pose the question to the family of the former owner–"were there any ghosts sighted there in their time?"

Blanche said the answer was "yes!"

"Their great-grandmother had been seen in the house after her death. She was a small, gray-haired, good-natured woman who just loved company, and who would probably have been delighted by the many people who visited Parastudy."

It could be that woman who has been seen in a third-floor bedroom, or on the main staircase over the years.

Those front stairs have been mentioned often in reports of the unusual.

On one occasion, a very young boy, the son of a member who had been at Parastudy for a covered dish supper, didn't know he was being observed when several people saw what they later

Ghost Stories of Delaware County

described:

The boy was climbing the front staircase on one of his many exploratory adventures in the house.

As he climbed the stairs, clinging to the banister, he was diverted toward the wall for a few steps as if he had encountered someone. Moments later, he came down the stairs and, at the very same location, was again detoured by the invisible force or being. That time, however, he also turned and mumbled something to whomever or whatever it was that he walked around.

Phantom footfalls have often been heard on those stairs, and disembodied conversations have been detected by many people, on many occasions, in many locations of the house.

Incidents there have not been limited to energies of the quiet variety. A former secretary told of a glass ashtray that literally "flew across" an upstairs bathroom.

A floor light in one room turned itself on on one occasion, and a couch pillow once was seen moving with no human assistance.

Blanche Biegenwald had her own chilling occurrence during one of the group's "Open House" events.

"A group of us was sitting around the kitchen table, just snacking and chatting, when *something*

Ghost Stories of Delaware County

grabbed the collar of my blouse. It brushed my hair lightly, as well. I turned around expectantly, to see who was behind me. Nobody was there.

"My reaction did not go unnoticed by those at the table, so I described what had just happened. 'Oh, that was M—, came the response from one of the members. 'She was always straightening your clothes, she was compulsive about neatness.' That member went on to tell me that M— had passed on the previous day!"

Blanche has collected other reports of unexplained incidents that range from the sensing of spirit pets to the muffled sounds of what appeared to be a veritable reunion of family ghosts.

"On Christmas Eve, 1974," she wrote, "the secretary reported, the house was very, very still. There had been neither visitors nor phone calls to mar the peace and quiet. At about two o'clock in the afternoon, she became aware of a great deal of activity. She felt the presence of a 'gathering of the clan' for the holidays. It seemed to be a very joyous reunion–children laughing and running up and down the back stairway. A great deal of bustle and activity centered in the pantry and around the area where the old cook stove once stood. She sensed the arrival of horses and carriages, and of their being taken into the carriage house.

Ghost Stories of Delaware County

"A little after three o'clock, the secretary bid 'them' farewell and a happy holiday, and drove home to finish her own Christmas preparations."

Latter-day "ghost hunters" and media investigators have descended upon the Parastudy house in search of anomalies and activity that might be detected electronically.

Using a toolbox of technical devices, the probers have recorded enough audio and visual evidence to conclude that something is awry within the walls of the house.

A local television crew, filming a guided tour of the building, managed to put together a 20-minute segment, but not without complications. A "flying orb" was noticed during an interview, the audio was lost at one point, and the video mysteriously streaked and went from color to black-and-white. The production company was baffled. Blanche was not.

"I'm tempted to speculate that the Parastudy "Ghost Contingent" had been doing their best to get into the act," she said.

•

Ghost Stories of Delaware County

THE PINK LADY
The ghost in the window of the Riverside Yacht Club

When they talk about the Pink Lady at the Riverside Yacht Club, they're not talking about a mixed drink.

They're talking about a ghost that's come to be known by that name, and she is well known by members of the club.

When researching a book about haunted places, we often go on old-fashioned hunches. Quite honestly, we are not beneath simply knocking on the door of a place that *looks* haunted and ask if it *is* haunted.

Ghost Stories of Delaware County

Such was the case when we knocked on the door of the Riverside Yacht Club in Essington and posed the question to the first person who greeted us.

It was Ralph Costello, who didn't disappoint us. "I've been here 37 years, and I've always heard of her. Whenever something strange happens here, we blame it on her. I can't say I've ever seen anything, but I know the story."

Mr. Costello said the ghost wears a long, pink dress. She is seen mostly on the second floor, and has even been spotted through the window from the outside.

"They told me that she was engaged to a sailor and he was killed. She died of a broken heart in the building," Costello added.

The RYC's building has quite a history. It was the physicians' residence of the "Lazaretto," the massive brick building next door.

The name is derived from St. Lazarus, and the ca. 1799 structure was the quarantine spot for Philadelphia-bound immigrants who had to be detained because of a contagious disease.

It was designed in the Georgian style after the Pennsylvania Hospital in Philadelphia, and was used as a quarantine house for more than 70 years. Inside, those afflicted with smallpox, yellow fever, and all sorts of other maladies were treated until

Ghost Stories of Delaware County

the federal government moved the quarantine operations to Marcus Hook. At its peak, the Lazaretto was a complex of seven buildings, including the physician's house. The main building enjoyed several decades as a resort for the rich, a seaplane base, and the centerpiece of a cluster of yacht clubs.

If any building truly "looked haunted," the Lazaretto does. However, no one of authority was available to address the issue on several visits there.

Another member of the Riverside Yacht Club, who asked to remain anonymous, said he had seen the "pink lady" of the club and believes the Lazaretto is also haunted.

"Our ghost is here all the time," he said of the pink lady. "And, there have been times when I just walked around or sat outside and looked at the Lazaretto and had a real sensation that there are ghosts in there. I'm not one to really believe in that sort of thing, but there's a feeling here that we're never really alone."

He said the "pink lady" ghost doesn't frighten him.

"She supposedly died of a broken heart," he said. "So, I guess her ghost is very sad and might just be looking for someone who cares about her."

Well said, sir. Well said.

Ghost Stories of Delaware County

REVOLUTIONARY WRAITHS
Do ghosts from earliest America haunt the Blue Bell Inn?

Only those with the most vivid imaginations could comprehend what happened at the Blue Bell

Ghost Stories of Delaware County

Inn, along Cobbs Creek where Philadelphia fades unceremoniously into Darby.

It didn't turn the tide of the war, it wasn't considered a major battle, but the 1777 encounter at the inn is a significant event in Delaware County history, even if the inn itself is within the city of Philadelphia.

After the Americans evacuated Fort Mifflin, a division of British soldiers, led by Lord Cornwallis, was marching out of Philadelphia toward Chester when they were met by about two dozen American pickets under the command of General Andrew Porter. The pickets had been in position at the Blue Bell Tavern.

The Americans were outnumbered by about one hundred to one. Of course, they knew they could not engage the British in battle, but they were there to torment and, at least momentarily, detain the troops as they made their way along the Great Southern Post Road.

Someone fired a shot, and a skirmish ensued. The Americans retreated into the Blue Bell. They positioned themselves at the windows and opened fire.

In the opening moments of the fight, two British soldiers, including the sergeant-major, were shot to death. Enraged, a horde of British Grenadiers stormed the inn and began a bloodbath.

Ghost Stories of Delaware County

They plunged their bayonets into the bellies of five Americans who rushed down the staircase. They shoved the bodies aside and climbed to the second floor, fully intending to massacre the entire band of Colonials. A British officer stepped in and ordered a halt to the attack. The rest of the Americans were captured alive.

In its prime, the inn was frequented by virtually every military, governmental, and civic leader of early America. George Washington stayed there on two documented occasions, and many legends have grown around the good times that were had there before and after the fatal skirmish.

But, other stories have been told about the ghosts that are said to dwell in the historic inn.

Darby historian John W. Haigis said it may well be a "Red Coat" who haunts the Blue Bell.

"A British soldier or officer was wounded," he said, "and brought into the Bell where his last words were 'I knew I would never leave this accursed land!' or words to that effect."

He cited former caretakers of the tavern who had personal–and frightening–experiences with the spirit there.

Or, make that *spirits*.

"There were two distinct ghosts there, with two distinct personalities," said David Sams, who

Ghost Stories of Delaware County

was caretaker at the Blue Bell from 1988 to 1997.

Sams believed one was the strong spirit of the British soldier. The other was a more pervasive, ambient energy that would be felt at any place and at any time in the building.

He recalled one incident that left him rattled.

"I was walking up the steps to the third floor, and I ran into something that made me feel as if I was walking into a freezer," he said. "My wife was right behind me, and she took a step up to where I had been and she felt it, too. I looked at her and something told me not to go any farther upstairs.

"Now, I've had other things happen to me over the years, but they didn't startle me. That time, on those stairs, it startled me."

Sams also remembered something that happened during a Civil War reenactment event on the grounds of the tavern.

"Someone took a picture, and a man's face was seen in a second-floor window. The thing is, there would have been no floor for that individual to be standing on. The floor had been burned away in a fire. It was impossible for someone to be up there, visible through that window. But, there it was, the clear-cut image of a man!"

Sams believes his wife, June, was more receptive to the energies in the Blue Bell, and for an interesting reason.

Ghost Stories of Delaware County

"She was born in Ireland," he noted, "and she seemed to think that the British soldier who haunts the place knew her to be a British subject."

June Sams added yet another character to the cast of spirits at the Blue Bell.

"I don't know who she is, but there's a woman there," she asserted.

"Once in awhile, I would smell the fragrance of roses there. And occasionally, I would feel a gentle hand on my shoulder. I never saw her, but I felt her presence."

She hesitates thinking about which ghost–the warrior or the woman–greeted her one night.

"I was awakened one night and felt a hand on my leg," she said, laughing nervously, "and it wasn't my husband's!"

Ravaged by time, vandalism, and arsonists over the years, the Blue Bell Tavern has nonetheless survived. At the time this book was being written, local preservationists had high hopes that it could be restored to its Colonial-era dignity.

John Haigis, who with his wife incorporated the "Friends of the Blue Bell" and who has served on the Darby Historic Commission, said he had never had a personal ghostly experience at the tavern, but said, "*something* has been looking out for the building for the past two and a half centuries."

Ghost Stories of Delaware County

THE WITCH OF RIDLEY CREEK
*Pennsylvania's only witchcraft trial
was held in Delaware County*

One would be hard-pressed these days to find exactly where she lived, but the only woman tried for witchcraft in Pennsylvania resided in what is now Delaware County.

According to a history of Eddystone, Margaret Mattson lived with her husband, Neels, on land that was part of the Baldwin Locomotive Plant grounds, somewhere east of Simpson Street.

The Mattsons owned vast acreage throughout the area, so the precise location of their home has become understandably unclear since the 1683

Ghost Stories of Delaware County

incident.

Margaret Mattson was accused of placing curses on a neighbor's cows and being possessed by demons.

Influential English settlers brought their complaints to the Provincial Council, chaired by William Penn.

Through translator Lasse Cock, a Swede who sat on the council, Mrs. Mattson pled "not guilty" to the charges.

After a review of the charges and testimony from both sides, the jury handed down an odd verdict. In the spelling and structure of the day, it read: *"Guilty of haveing the Comon fame of a witch, but not guilty in manner and forme as Shee stand Indicted."*

A legend has been passed on over the centuries regarding the trial and William Penn's simple question to Mrs. Mattson:

It is said that Penn asked the woman if, indeed, she was a witch and if she had ever ridden through the air on a broomstick.

Confused, Margaret answered, "yes."

Noting that there was no law against riding through the air on a broomstick, he recommended acquittal.

Or, so it is said.

•

Ghost Stories of Delaware County

THE WHITE LADY OF ESSINGTON

Bride who died on her wedding night is said to haunt a roadway near Philadelphia International Airport

A story has been told for many years about the tragic death of a young couple on Tinicum Island Road near the Philadelphia International Airport.

They were newlyweds, on the way from their wedding reception in Essington to the airport and their honeymoon.

It was a dark, foggy night. As careful as they may have been, they never saw the car coming from the opposite direction veer into their lane and smash into them head-on.

The groom was killed instantly, but the bride was thrown from the vehicle. Critically injured, she struggled with all her failing strength to summon someone, anyone, for help.

It is said that despite suffering two broken legs, the young woman crawled and stumbled

Ghost Stories of Delaware County

several yards from the scene of the collision until death claimed her pain-wracked body.

It wasn't until the following morning that the bodies of the groom, the driver of the other vehicle, and the bride were discovered by a passing motorist.

From that day to the present, legend has it that the bride's ghost appears as a battered body dressed in a bloody wedding gown, along a certain stretch of the road.

She has been seen as a misty form, or as a horrid vision that appears and disappears in the blink of an eye.

Richard Grosso, of Darby, had heard the stories about what most folks called "The White Lady." And, on one late night on Tinicum Island Road, he feels he saw her.

"I was on my way home, and the only light on the road was a streetlight. I saw a lady, dressed in white, standing under the light."

He passed so quickly that he couldn't discern many details of her mode of dress.

"At first I thought it was a real person," he said. "I went down the road, turned around, but she had vanished."

"I didn't believe or not believe in the 'White Lady,'" he added, "until that night."

Now, he believes.

Ghost Stories of Delaware County

The "Lydia Room" at the Crier in the Country

HAUNTED RESTAURANTS REVISITED

Updates on two Delaware County restaurants featured in a previous publication

Four years before this book was conceived, I wrote and Exeter House Books published *Ghost Stories of Chester County and the Brandywine Valley*.

Quite honestly, a book about haunted places in Delaware County wasn't even on the drawing

Ghost Stories of Delaware County

boards at that time. Although we are normally very provincial in our research and stop at the border lines of each county we have featured in this series of books, the Chester County book was expanded a bit to include the Brandywine Valley which, of course, extends into Delaware County.

A handful of stories in the Chester County book actually took place at sites in Delaware County. Two of them merit review and updates in this volume.

One was a story we called "The Singing Spirit of Hurricane Hill."

It is set in the Crier in the Country restaurant, along Route 1 in Glen Mills.

It is the haunt–literally–of Lydia Powel, for whom one of the upstairs rooms at the Crier was named.

Lydia lived there with her husband for about twelve years in the mid-1800s. According to many reports over the years, she may "live" there still today.

At least two generations of owners of the stately restaurant have felt and often seen her presence there, often in the room that bears her name.

Mysterious flashes of light, the sounds of soft singing, and full apparitions of an elegant but somber woman have been seen throughout the

Ghost Stories of Delaware County

spacious and well-appointed mansion by many patrons and staff members.

For an update on the story, we turn to Laurie Hull, of the Delaware County Paranormal group, who visited the Crier in the Country to see (and hear) for herself if Lydia was still active there.

"I have had so many experiences here, and the restaurant is so rich in history," she said, "I barely know where to start!"

She started with some of the more recent ramblings of Lydia, but continued with other apparitions that have been detected there.

"The spirit of a young woman is said to frequent the area of the downstairs women's restroom," she said. "She startles people, but like Lydia, seems content to just watch the activity going on without interacting with the current residents and visitors. It has been said that this restroom ghost is the spirit of Lydia's daughter."

On one visit to the restaurant, Laurie and a companion watched in awe as something appeared to them in front of the building.

"My dinner partner and I kept seeing someone in white walk by on the front porch. We asked the waitress if anyone was out there, and she said 'No.' We saw the figure a few more times, and got up to investigate ourselves, but there was no one there."

Ghost Stories of Delaware County

Another superb restaurant in Delaware County is the Chadds Ford Inn, where three very active spirits hold fort.

They are "Katie," "Simon," and "The Sea Captain," and this writer can vouch for each of their presences.

Actually, ghost probers and sensitive staffers have detected many "hot spots" of ghostly energies in the ancient and historic inn. Strange occurrences, radical temperature and pressure variations, and other unexpected and unexplainable incidents are experienced there constantly.

But, the "big three" ghosts at the Chadds Ford Inn are very likely to be detected by someone with even the lowest level of sensitivity to the supernatural.

Simon is a little boy wearing bloomer pants and a ruffled shirt. He is most likely to be found at the top of the main staircase that leads to the second floor dining rooms.

Look for Katie almost anywhere in the building. She seems to have free reign there, and has been seen or sensed by many in the waitstaff and several diners.

The Sea Captain favors one particular table at a second floor window, but has also been seen in the second floor hallway and on the staircase, motioning as if he is lighting a pipe.

Ghost Stories of Delaware County

The names of each of the ghosts at Chadds Ford are purely arbitrary, and there is scarce historical evidence that would provide baselines for their eternal existence there.

I can confirm, however, that the ghosts of both the Crier in the Country and the Chadds Ford Inn are very real–if "real" is an operative word in this case.

Over the years, I have been privileged to present ghost storytelling sessions at both restaurants, and I have actually been interrupted by the manifestations of the spirits there. Nothing untoward or at all threatening ever took place, but there was no doubt in my mind that the gathering of the willing and the telling of the stories seemed to stir the ethereal emotions of the energies there.

On several occasions, I noticed individuals or groups reacting oddly or warily as they walked through certain areas or sat at certain tables in both restaurants. It was only when I told my stories and pinpointed the known "hot spots" that they realized they had been in the midst of the energies and may have been visited by the spirits.

Once, I was in the middle of a story on the second floor of the Chadds Ford Inn when a very clear and present force made its way slowly through the room, weaving from table to table and actually rattling a door that leads to the third floor of the building.

The owners of both the Crier in the Country and the Chadds Ford Inn cannot and do not deny the preponderance of evidence that leads them to concede that their establishments are inhabited by inocuous but ubiqitous entities.

Indeed, having their own ghostly experiences and stories to tell, these restaurateurs have embraced the spirits as contributors to the overall character of their historic establishments.

(NOTE: As this book was going to press in spring, 2005, the Chadds Ford Inn had closed for renovations.)

•

HEDGING ON HAUNTINGS

"There's always a surmise that this is a haunted building," said Zoran Kovcic, "but apparently it is not."

The operations manager of Hedgerow Theatre in Rose Valley said that despite the outward appearance of the theater, there have been only scant reports of any kinds of ghostly activity there.

But, Hedgerow House, the actors' late-Victorian style residence along Rose Valley Road, houses a veritable "parade of spirits," as one former tenant described it.

"He claimed there are all kinds of spirits there," Kovcic continued. "The barn is next to a graveyard that dates to the Revolutionary War time. He claimed there is a slave graveyard there, and that some of their ghosts would walk around there."

The former resident also mentioned the presence of a little girl who would appear at a certain window and peer aimlessly into the building.

Ghost Stories of Delaware County

The Manor

GHOSTS OF THE GREEK HOUSES

It is no secret that at least two of the many stately, old buildings on the campus of Widener University have long histories of hauntings.

The tales have been detailed in student handbooks, and they now appear on the

Ghost Stories of Delaware County

university's official web site.

The two most storied "haunted houses" at Widener stand across from one another at 14th and Potter Streets. They are the sorority houses of Delta Psi Epsilon ("The Castle") and Phi Sigma Sigma ("The Manor").

The Castle (above) dates to 1913 and is haunted by an unidentified spirit or spirits that often create "cold spots" throughout its rooms, corridors, and staircases.

A security patrolman at Widener said he has certainly heard of the reports of ghostly activity in The Castle, and has even felt the "cold spots" himself. When asked the direct question, "Do you

Ghost Stories of Delaware County

think it's haunted?" he shrugged, winced, and offered no personal opinion. "But," he conceded, "there have been many, *many* reports of it coming from out of it, so who am I to say?"

He, and another security guard at the university, noted that they have responded to–sometimes with city of Chester police–to calls to The Castle that turn up nothing but are later attributed to "the ghost."

Across the street looms the sturdy former Woodbridge Estate, nicknamed "The Manor."

The ghost there has speculatively named "Louise," as in Louise Deshong Woodbridge (1848-1925), who lived there with her husband, Jonathan.

Louise was a member of the wealthy and influential Deshong family, whose largesse and legacies are intertwined with the history of Widener University.

Sorority sisters of Phi Sigma Sigma have long heard, seen, felt, and smelled the vestiges of Louise Woodbridge.

One current resident said "there is no doubt whatsoever" to her that a ghost dwells within the solid walls of the mansion.

The aroma of fresh baked goods has often been detected in the building, when nobody is baking.

Ghost Stories of Delaware County

"I heard some girls say they've heard the muffled sound of a dog barking, or felt the brush of a dog's fur against their legs," the resident said.

"Some girls say they have even seen the ghost of a lady, like out of the Victorian age or something, standing or walking around the house," she continued.

"It can get a little creepy in here," she added. "I mean, it's a great house and all, but just look at it! It looks like it should be haunted.

"The worst time is at Halloween, when a lot of strange things seem to happen. I don't know for sure, but I was told that the former owner of the house died on Halloween. Now, that would *really* be creepy if it was really true."

It is true. Louise Deshong Woodbridge died in The Castle in the early morning hours of Halloween, 1925.

According to legend, as Louise lay dying, she vowed to never leave her beloved home–or her beloved dog.

Perhaps she never has.

•

HUP, TWO...THREE...BOO!

What is now the Widener University campus was once the Pennsylvania Military College. It has been reported that ghostly forms of PMC-uniformed students have been spotted at various locations at Widener.

Ghost Stories of Delaware County

THE HAMANASSETT HAUNTING
Do ghosts mingle with guests at a luxurious Brandywine Valley B&B?

In the course of researching this book, I sent emails to country inns, restaurants, and bed & breakfasts throughout Delaware County. My question was to the point, something like this: "Are there any stories of hauntings or reports of ghosts being sighted in your establishment?"

"As to your question about ghosts here," replied Ashley Mon, "I have to say I'm not sure."

Ashley is the owner and innkeeper of the lovely Hamanassett Bed & Breakfast on Indian Springs Drive, Chester Heights.

Built in 1856 of native fieldstone by the Dr. Charles Meigs, president of the Royal College of Physicians, Hamanassett was intended to be his country retreat and retirement residence. Unfortunately, he passed away before those dreams could come true.

In the early years of the 20th century, Joseph

Ghost Stories of Delaware County

The Windsor Room at the Hamanassett B&B

Ghost Stories of Delaware County

Dohan, a Philadelphia attorney and owner of the Glen Mills Paper Company, renovated the main house and expanded it to the Federalist style it now represents. The Lima Hunt was headquartered there, and fox hunters from around the world gathered on its vast acreage.

That acreage was pared down after Dohan's death when his wife, Dr. Edith Dohan, sold about 300 acres to satisfy tax claims. Dr. Dohan also then changed her name back to her maiden name and continued her career as a world-renowned archaeologist and Curator of the Classics at the University of Pennsylvania Museum.

With a pedigree such as that, Hamanassett is sure to have many stories to tell. Perhaps someone from its storied past is trying to do just that.

Ashley said she has had some "odd experiences," but it is her beloved Doberman "Regal," who may be most sensitive to the energies in the majestic mansion.

"She runs around the house and up and down the stairs all the time," Ashley said. "However, every so often, always late at night and always when I am here alone, she will stop at the first landing and cry and whimper but will not come down. I have to go up and take her by the collar and walk down with her."

Ashley and her husband, Glenn, had owned a

Ghost Stories of Delaware County

bed and breakfast in New Orleans prior to purchasing the Hamanassett in 2001. They knew the idiosyncracies of both properties and patrons. But, no innkeeper is totally prepared to deal with the prospect of spirits within their midst.

On one occasion, a guest asked Ashley about any ghosts that might haunt the Hamanassett. "I told her the story about our dog and she told me she thought I have a presence who only comes out when I'm alone, to look over me and keep me company."

Three different couples who have stayed there have actually reported incidents.

"They each said they felt a presence in their room," Ashley said. "One man claimed he saw a woman, but I can't remember what else he said. What is interesting is that every couple was sleeping in the same room, the Windsor."

Accented by an ten-foot tall antique Half Tester rosewood bed from a Louisiana plantation and appointed with both vintage furniture and modern amenities, the Windsor is one of six rooms in the main house (there is a two-story detached Carriage House with more accommodations) and is typical of the elegantly comfortable bedchambers there.

There is a sense of serenity in that room, and those who possess the ability to "read" spirit

Ghost Stories of Delaware County

activity and understand its usually benign nature, have been at one with what seems to be a feminine spirit there.

Interestingly, Ashley Mon discovered that in the 1896 plans of the mansion, what is now the Windsor Room was divided as two separate rooms.

In virtually every case investigated or observed by this writer, ghostly activity seems to be stirred or generated during or following renovations or revisions to a building's structure.

It is as if the removal or addition of a wall, window, door, or floor may somehow alter the path or motion of resident energies and cause them to create sights, sounds, and sensations that had been contained and controlled with the bounds that those energies, those *ghosts*, once knew.

There is another possibility, another theory that energies may well be transported and transplanted into a property via furniture, tools, and other items and implements.

I call it the "rusty nail" theory.

If, as I believe, what we call "ghosts" are little more than manifestations of energies deposited by the release of those energies at the time of one's passing, I also believe it is possible that those energies could "record" themselves on some sort of storage medium.

And if, as I believe and some research has

seemed to support, those energies are of an electrical nature, that medium could be something as simple as rust.

Think of it as sound or electrical impulses recording on audio or video tape.

Tape is nothing more than iron and ferric oxide–rust. A recording is made when an electromagnet converts the impulses it receives into the recorded product.

That recording is played back through another magnetic process.

Although items around any house, wires and cables over any house, and other external influences may be disruptive, it could be that the magnetic fields of certain areas we then call "haunted" are actually the storage media for those energies from a past life. And, it could be that one of those media could be something as simple as rust.

The rust may be geological, or on an item within the walls of the structure. It could be a rusty hinge, beam, or nail.

What's more, it could be on something that has nothing to do with the property. The rust, with the recorded energies, could be on an item that was brought into the house.

"This is interesting," said Ashley Mon of the possible correlation between the "rusty nail theory"

Ghost Stories of Delaware County

and the perceived energy in the Windsor Room.

"I never considered that perhaps the bed came with a presence. It came from a plantation outside of New Orleans."

With that, Ashley displayed insight, understanding, and inquisitiveness that is rare and refreshing.

So, how could something as inocuous and invisible as energy recorded on rust–or whatever storage medium–become a ghost?

Could it not be that those shards of information and emotion, those bits and pieces of audible and visual signals, are there, forever there, for those with the inborn or electronic equipment to discover and define them?

And, could it not be that the stored, recorded energies are "played back" by individuals with psychic abilities and/or detected by "ghost hunters" with electromagnetic field meters?

A friend who has studied the paranormal, actively investigated hauntings for many years, and managed ghost tours in Gettysburg, once posed a provocative question during a discussion of psychic and scientific "ghost hunting."

The discussion was of orbs and apparitions, EVPs and ESP, ghost hunting and ghost debunking.

"Who decided," she said quizically, "that orbs

Ghost Stories of Delaware County

are ghostly energies or that 'hot spots,' 'cold spots,' or glitches in the electromagnetic field have anything whatsoever to do with past lives?"

Indeed. The is no answer, and I dearly desire that there never be an answer.

Do ghosts exist?

In the more than a quarter of a century that I have been writing about ghosts and haunted places, and considering the dozens of times I have had personal encounters with the unexplained, I still force myself to remain unconvinced that the dead walk among the living.

Frankly, I don't want to know. I don't want to live in a world in which that question has been answered with some finality.

Do ghosts exist?

It is one of the last questions we may debate as a society, one of the last questions that sparks not only controversy and ridicule, but something much more valuable to every one of us. It sparks something that has been stripped nearly bare by science and reality. It sparks the imagination.

When children can no longer cringe at ghost stories told at a campfire, when adults can no longer cower on the couch while watching a scary ghost movie, we have lost a precious and irretrievable human trait...the ability to *wonder*.

•

Ghost Stories of Delaware County

COLONIAL GHOSTS
Do spirits linger at the Colonial Pennsylvania Plantation?

Do ghostly carriages and buggies traverse what is in essence a "ghost road" at the Colonial Pennsylvania Plantation?

What mysterious force blocked a woman's passage down a staircase there? Does a phantom figure dwell on the dark steps that lead to the root cellar?

These and many more questions are waiting to be answered as volunteers and farm workers at the plantation continue to gather evidence that leads several of them to believe the historic farmstead is haunted.

Ghost Stories of Delaware County

Colonial Pennsylvania Plantation is an independent, nonprofit organization that leases land from the commonwealth's Bureau of State Parks. It is situated in a 112-acre corner of Ridley Creek State Park and is a faithful reproduction of a working 18th century farm.

Volunteers continue time-honored tasks throughout the buildings and on the land, and tour guides present realistic interpretations of how the Joseph Pratt family–the farm's 18th century owners–lived, worked, and played on their property.

Archaeologists have determined that a structure existed on the site as early as 1705. Joseph Pratt moved there in 1720 and immediately expanded that first house to accommodate his family's needs.

A series of modifications continued through the late 18th century until the proportions now seen were reached around 1830. Specifically, the present building outwardly resembles its 1830 appearance, but the interior appointments and furnishings are more in tune with what it would have looked like in 1775.

Among the most popular yearly events at the Plantation are the ghost tours each fall. The storytellers need not look far for inspiration.

Spirit activity has been reported inside and

Ghost Stories of Delaware County

just outside the farmhouse by many people for many years.

To the rear of the house is an old roadway, used only occasionally these days. In olden days, it was used often by wagons pulled by teams of horses. One woman who has been volunteering at the Plantation for more than two decades, said it is a "very common" occurrence for workers and volunteers there to hear the muffled but distinct sound of horses' hooves and the crush of wagon wheels on gravel, as if phantom wagons still pass by. She ventured that, indeed, *most* people there have at one time or another heard the sound of the wagons on the road, just up the hill from the house.

Some have heard the sound and looked quickly to see the fleeting shadowy forms accompany the sound.

In the house itself are many spots where ghosts are believed to linger. A second floor room, over the kitchen, is used by guides and historical interpreters to change into their 18th century costumes. Often, in the hottest heat of summer, eerie, icy pockets of air materialize mysteriously. The phenomenon is often associated with the presence of a ghost.

One volunteer was vexed by a peculiar incident as she was descending a staircase from the

Ghost Stories of Delaware County

third floor in the oldest section of the house.

She was carrying a load of items when she was stymied by a force that seemed to anchor her foot on the step. She knew it was not a physical impairment and immediately attributed it to the presence of an unseen energy. Instinctively, she asserted loudly and clearly that she was not removing anything from the house, not damaging anything, just taking it from one place to another.

Suddenly, as if the force understood and accepted her plea, her foot moved once more.

Another volunteer will never forget and will forever be both amused and confused by a case that involved a package of cleaning cloths.

She had brought the package into the farmhouse for future use. When the time came to use the cloths, they were nowhere to be found. She knew where she had placed them, but they were gone.

She was miffed, but the matter eventually faded into memory. Until, that is, the cleaning cloths reappeared–in a freezer!

If there are no ghosts, no spirits from the past at a place so steeped in the heritage of Delaware County and so treasured by those who have restored and maintain it, an element of its very character would be missing.

The Plantation and the parklands around it are

Ghost Stories of Delaware County

an appealing blend of a lot of history and a little mystery.

The main road that courses through Ridley Creek Park and to the Colonial Plantation is Sandy Flash Road. It was named after the notorious 18th century outlaw who was hanged on "Gallows Hill" in Chester in 1778.

The Philadelphia Ghost Hunters Alliance and a Philadelphia radio station staged two ghost hunts at the Plantation in recent years, and the Plantation was chosen by renowned moviemaker M. Night Shyamalan as the site of what was called an "historic boot camp" for the cast of "The Village," when it was filmed nearby in 2003. They learned and performed household and farming tasks that were germane to their roles and the plot of the movie.

Someone once warmed my heart when they told me that as I investigate and chronicle the past lives, loves, dramas and traumas that have played out in haunted places I am "reading the souls of houses."

At Colonial Pennsylvania Plantation, you, too, will be in the heart of history, able to read the soul of the house and its grounds.

And perhaps, a spirit or two will manifest to add yet another element to a day down on this most marvelous farm.

Ghost Stories of Delaware County

The Heilbron Mansion, ca. 1950
Photo courtesy of East Coast Productions, LLC and Dan Diehl

STILL STALKED BY GHOSTS?
The Heilbron Mansion ghosts–fact or fiction?

What is probably the most famous haunted house in Delaware County history is itself a ghost.

It was the Heilbron Mansion, and it was the subject of the 1977 National Writer's Club Award for *nonfiction*, "Night Stalks the Mansion," by Constance Westbie and Harold Cameron.

Note the accent on *nonfiction*.

The book chronicles the unearthly events experienced over a two-year period by the Cameron family in the house on Rose Tree Road in Middletown Township.

On June 4, 1987, the mansion was reduced to

Ghost Stories of Delaware County

rubble by an arsonist. It was the final, tragic blow to what was once the 17-room stone manor house of a splendid 150-year old estate that spread over 100 acres and included four substantial buildings.

At the time of its loss, the mansion had been vacant for more than two years. It was during that time that vandals, looters, and thrill-seekers ripped the house to shreds.

Many years passed after the publication of the book and destruction of the property, but interest in the supernatural stories that emerged from the mansion did not fade.

"Harold Cameron died of cancer in 1984," said Dan Diehl, Cameron's grandnephew and the man who was the driving force behind the book's re-release by Stackpole Books in 2005. "All but one of Harold's siblings have died as well, but many of his children and extended family survive today."

At the time of the writing of *Ghost Stories of Delaware County*, Diehl was also negotiating with producers and studio executives in Los Angeles to bring the Heilbron Mansion story to the big screen.

"Three years ago," he continued, "I was looking for a project that would be more challenging than what I was doing at the time. I glanced up at my bookshelf and saw the original hardback book written by my great-uncle. I had

Ghost Stories of Delaware County

thumbed through the book often over the years, but this time I picked it up and didn't put it down until I had read it cover to cover. At that moment, something sparked inside me: I decided that I wanted to make a movie script based on the book.

"Determined to succeed, I gathered a small group of colleagues together to discuss the idea, and everyone loved it. Lucky for me, there was no option on the book, so I was able to secure it and write my script.

"While I was writing the script, I was able to fly to Philadelphia with my co-writer, John Barker to see for myself what remained of the mansion. It was snowing and dismal when we arrived in Philadelphia and we immediately set out to find the mansion.

"Amazingly, it was a short trip to Media ("Wynn" in the book), so we were very excited that we would be able to see the mansion before dark. As we drove, we could immediately see why this would be the perfect place for a haunted house.

"We met each hill with anticipation looking for a huge stone mansion that we thought would look like the old photos we had found.

"Sadly, when we finally crossed the bridge and saw the mansion perched in a hill in the distance, we were disappointed because virtually

Ghost Stories of Delaware County

nothing was as we thought it would be. Don't get me wrong, it was absolutely beautiful, but that is not what we wanted to find. Furthermore, all the outbuildings and landscape features mentioned in the book were either gone or unrecognizable. Everything had been developed and what used to be 100 acres of farmland is now a sprawling subdivision.

"As we stared at the new facade, it was apparent that only the stone walls and foundation remained from the original mansion.

"After that, we decided to continue on our path of finding any references to the history of the mansion and what we found was incredible. The most impressive things we found were the postcard that Harold wrote about in the book, a yellowed photograph of the entire facade of the mansion as it looked around the time Harold lived there and historical documents of all the buildings on the property at the time Harold lived there including the mansion, barn and the springhouse!

"We were also able to meet and interview Harold's son, Carol Cameron, who was around 12 when he lived in the mansion and has several strange experiences documented in the book. Carol retired as the art director for the Department for Housing and Urban Development.

"He graciously answered all the questions we

Ghost Stories of Delaware County

asked him and even drew floor plans of the mansion as he remembered it. During the visit, he showed me his office where he had photos and drawings mounted all over the wall. He pointed for me to look closer at some of them so I did. There on the wall of a cousin I had never met were photos of my grandmother, uncles and other family members! It was at that moment that I realized that what I was doing was for a purpose."

Laurie Hull, of the Delaware County Paranormal Research group, said that she had been to the mansion during its dying dormancy.

She was 16 at the time, and was not comfortable as she and a group of friends "visited" the place.

As her friends explored the upper floors of the house, Laurie remained just inside the front door.

"Suddenly," she said, "I heard a tremendous crash. It sounded as if someone had dropped a truckload of aluminum cans onto the roof of the house and let them roll all over. I dashed out the front door, off the porch, and hit the ground running. My friends were not far behind!"

Carolyn Sullivan was another of those who gave in to temptation and went on the prowl in the Heilbron Mansion.

"It was 1986, and it was still standing, a half-

Ghost Stories of Delaware County

boarded up eyesore," she wrote in an email.

"Local kids told stories that it was haunted and it was a popular place to go with a bunch of friends, to spook yourselves out. The stories all conflicted, though, so I researched at a local library, found the book, grew incredibly curious, and had to check it out for myself.

"So, one night, my friends and I grabbed a bunch of flashlights and, under the cover of darkness, climbed in through the one big unboarded window to look around.

"Immediately, I knew we were in the living room of the house that the book described in such detail. I easily located the main staircase. and found the library. 'This is the library,' I said, 'the center of the hauntings.' Our flashlight beams zipped fearlessly around the room and a few of us made mock-spooky *'ooooh...ahhhh'* sounds."

As they were horsing around with their flashlights, every one of the lights turned off, without human aid.

"I almost wet my pants," Carolyn continued. "In total darkness, we all screamed and ran around bumping into each other and waving our flashlights in the air. Eventually, they all blinked back on so we could hightail it out of there without killing ourselves. Safe in the car, on the way home, we all agreed something beyond clear explanation happened."

In her communiqué, sent years before any book about Delaware County ghost stories was considered by this writer, Carolyn summed up her thoughts after that simple, but harrowing experience.

"Sure, it could have been a coincidence," she admitted. "Sure, our flashlights all might have been dying out after wandering around the house so long.

"I don't really know what happened, and to this day I'm not totally convinced it was a paranormal experience. However, it's fun to think that maybe, just maybe, 'the lady' was there, watching us, and she had the last laugh!"

Long before the Westbie/Cameron book was written, the Heilbron Mansion had been rumored to be haunted. Depending on the "source" you choose, its ghostly inhabitants included a farm worker who was hanged in the front yard after he raped and murdered the teenage daughter of the property owner, the murdered girl, and the girl's mother who was so grief-stricken that she hanged herself from a beam in an upper-floor room.

Township and county historians have not found any credible documentation for the baseline event that would support the rape-murder-lynching-suicide story.

Ghost Stories of Delaware County

The book based the haunting on the crime that took place in 1864 and involved a 14-year old girl.

Researchers did concede that based on census records, the home's builder, Joseph Edwards, would have had a 14-year old daughter named Margaret in 1864 and records also revealed that a 30-year old farmhand named Elisha Culbert lived there at that time.

There is, however, no record of any crimes there in that year.

But, several historians do agree that such a heinous series of events may well have been "hushed up" and left unrecorded. They also admit that the property had a haunted reputation at least as far back as the turn of the 20th century.

So, should "Night Stalks the Mansion" be in the fiction or nonfiction shelves of a book store?

Does it matter?

The property is now part of a sprawling community of luxury homes. When the developers plotted the subdivision, they knew the stories of the ghosts but determined them to be distractions and detractions from the historic character of the land.

Do more than just old ghost stories stalk the land where the Heilbron Mansion once stood?

That's a question only the present occupants of that land can answer.

Ghost Stories of Delaware County

Sweetwater Farm B&B

THE NOCTURNAL PRANKSTER OF SWEETWATER FARM

Oh, the tales the walls could tell at the Sweetwater Farm Bed & Breakfast near Glen Mills.

They would tell stories not only of distant history but of more recent events that have caused it to be called "Hollywood on the Brandywine."

The property has been witness to the rage of the American Revolution, the refuge of the Underground Railroad, and untold events that have unfolded inside and around it.

It earned its movie-associated moniker when it was chosen by M. Night Shyamalan to house the

Ghost Stories of Delaware County

cast of "The Village" during the two months it was filmed nearby in 2003.

The producer/director housed his actors and actresses in a period place, said Sweetwater Farm B&B owner Chris Le Vine, "because he didn't want his cast to go from a Ritz-Carlton to 1898 and back during the filming."

Le Vine and his wife, Vicky, have owned the B&B since 1999. And, Chris has other connections with Hollywood. His aunt was the late Philadelphia-born actress Grace Kelly, as in Princess Grace of Monaco. His cousin, as in Princess Caroline, has stayed at the B&B, and the photographs of other luminaries who have been guest there adorn the walls of the reception area.

People and property pedigrees aside, the manor house features three rooms in the oldest section, some of which dates to 1734; four more rooms in the ca. 1815 wing; and five more rooms in the adjacent cottages on the 50-acre farm. Each room has its own elegant individuality.

One of those rooms may also have its own eternal resident.

"We do have some unusual occurrences in the old side of the house," said Chris Le Vine.

One very unusual occurrence–or, more properly–*occurrences* took place in the Dormer Room, a chamber tucked cozily under the roof of

Ghost Stories of Delaware County

the original fieldstone farmhouse. Legend has it that it was a secret infirmary for runaway slaves when the farm was a "station" on the Underground Railroad.

"There were actually two guests in the Dormer Room, on two separate occasions, who felt that somebody was yanking their bed covers in the middle of the night," Le Vine continued.

"Now, when two of them said the exact same thing, that caught my attention."

Although there is no historical documentation to back up any imprinting of ghostly energy at Sweetwater Farm, there is speculation that the nocturnal prankster is a child.

"It just seems that it would be something a young child would do," said Le Vine. "You know, just playing little games, having a little fun."

Playful prank or not, Le Vine did admit that another couple actually did emerge from the room one night about 11 o'clock and announced that they could not stay in the Dormer Room.

"They told us they were spooked in that room," Le Vine said.

The couple was offered another room, where they enjoyed a restful night.

•

Ghost Stories of Delaware County

AND, IN THE END....
Art imitates death in a Drexel Hill Cemetery

Death is a fact of life. And, there's that old adage, "The only two certainties in life are death and taxes."

In Delaware County there is no museum dedicated to paying or collecting taxes, but–you guessed it–there is a museum which centers on that final step toward the great beyond.

Actually, the collections at Arlington Cemetery in Drexel Hill make up the Museum of Mourning Art, and thus is a tribute not to death, but to how survivors deal with it.

What could be a morbid place is surprisingly bright and expectedly dignified.

The museum is set within the 200-acre cemetery's central building, which is a dead-ringer,

Ghost Stories of Delaware County

so to speak, for Mount Vernon.

Appropriately, a good portion of the collection focuses on the death of and grieving for George Washington.

The passing of America's first real national hero in December 1799 was a pivotal point in the history of the young nation and touched off what could be considered modern American mourning art.

The occasion left a stunning legacy of paintings, engravings, sculpture and jewelry.

In the museum is a display case with a Currier and Ives print of Washington, a Wedgwood bust, and a leather box with a pearl-and-gold ring.

Adorning the ring are locks of hair which are believed to have been cut from the head of Washington after his death.

The ring was one of five which were distributed to Washington's immediate relatives following his death.

Such was a common practice. These "mourning rings" were prepared by jewelers with hair provided by morticians.

The museum collection predates American mourning art, with its oldest artifact dating to the 16th century.

A replica of Albrecht Durer's "Melancolia I," which was used to illustrate the fragile connection

Ghost Stories of Delaware County

between life and death, is a prime example, as are 200-year old Pennsylvania German prints by Christian Peters.

It was in these early centuries that the most maudlin and frightening images of death were conveyed on tombstones, broadsides and death announcements.

Perhaps even more ominous is an exhibit which includes a small cannon that was used by cemetery sentries.

As medical experimentation matured, Frankensteinian doctors would pay grave robbers to steal corpses from cemeteries. Many cemeteries were forced to post armed guards to ward off the cadaver thieves.

Attitudes about death and the mourning process shifted in the latter part of the 18th century. Horrid skulls were replaced by cherubic angels in death emblems, and funerals became celebrations of the deceased's life, not death.

An 1890 hearse, made by Sayers and Scovill of Cincinnati, is the centerpiece of the museum. The ornate vehicle exemplifies the Victorian approach to death and its aftermath.

Throughout the museum, the collection reinforces the evolution of society's ambivalence about death through art.

The museum at Arlington Cemetery opened in

Ghost Stories of Delaware County

September 1990. Associated with Princeton University Center of Theological Inquiry, the museum carefully depicts the sometimes subtle, sometimes radical shifts in the perceptions of death.

The dawn of the age of science cast long shadows on the grip religion held on the mourning process.

It wasn't until the late 1700s that the notion of providing comfort to grieving survivors took hold.

That meant the end of much of the elaborate art commissioned for funereal purposes.

Or did it?

There has been a resurgence in mourning art in recent decades.

The transfer of ancient tombstone epitaphs by "rubbing" them has become a minor art form. And, new technology employed by monument makers has created a rebirth of elaborate gravestone markers.

The exhibits at this most unusual museum conclude, appropriately, with a display of artwork associated with the death of the evangelist Rev. George Whitfield in Philadelphia in 1770.

As for this story, it shall end with words which befit both the allotment of space on this page and the subject matter...

THE END

Ghost Stories of Delaware County

•APPENDIX•
A GHOST HUNTER'S GLOSSARY

Information compiled by Justin Faulk,
http://ghostgadgets.com   Used with permission.

Anomaly
Something found with no explainable source. An unexplainable source of data.

Apparition
The most rare of all photographic anomalies, this is actually capturing a manifestation on film. An apparition is a spirit that has taken human form, and has come down to a wavelength visible to infrared based cameras, and/or the human eye. Sometimes they are visible to the human eye, and

Ghost Stories of Delaware County

sometimes they are not. Usually associated with energy lights, these are very rare indeed.

Cameras and Audio Recorders

Obviously, to take paranormal photos and record EVP you need a camera and an audio recorder. Digital cameras are used many times by investigators, but it is inexpensive to take thousands of photos and you get instant results, unlike 35mm film, that is expensive to develop and you have to wait several days for it to develop. The main problem with digital is you have no negative, so it is harder to prove your photo wasn't faked. You can get results on either type of camera, though.

Ectoplasm & Misting

Usually shows up looking like smoke or fog in photos. It is a mist that usually isn't visible at the time the photo is taken, but can fill whole areas without you even knowing it.

EMF Meter

EMF Meters measure electromagnetic fields. Spirits have been found to sometimes disturb or create their own electromagnetic field, which can be found with these meters. When no explainable source can be found for an EMF, it is said to be an EMF anomaly, and spirit activity could be present. A moving field, or spike in the EMF field could

Ghost Stories of Delaware County

represent spirit activity, too.
Note: Power lines, electrical appliances, and other common household items put out EMFs, so be sure that when you discover an EMF, you don't jump to conclusions and say it is a ghost!

Energy Lights

These are usually associated with a manifestation of some sort, and show up in photos as colored lights. Energy lights are usually not visible to the naked eye at the time the photo is taken. The ones I have taken and seen have all been of an orange color, and sometimes even take the shape of an apparition, or part of an apparition.

EVP (Electronic Voice Phenomenon)

Probably one of the most compelling of paranormal phenomena. When you record audio, and at playback you discover voices that could not be heard at the time of recording, and that have no explainable source. Some investigators ask questions to see if they can get responses, and others just prefer to record the whole investigation, and see what they came up with later. Some will tell you that tape recorders work better than digital, but I have found that a good digital recorder works just as well, if not better.

Intelligent Haunting

When spirits seem to live in a specific area, and

Ghost Stories of Delaware County

act with free will, as well as show intelligence (i.e.: not residual). Spirits don't necessarily haunt the place they died, but could haunt the most comfortable place for them to stay (i.e.: their old home). We are not quite sure why these spirits remain earthbound.

Kinetic Energy

When spirits use their energy to move objects, throw things, etc. This is very interesting phenomena, and personally, I have had rocks thrown at me by an unseen force, and have witnessed equipment actually being struck and broken by unseen forces.

Motion Detectors

Some investigators use motion detectors to monitor any unseen heat movement or object movement.

Orb

A form of energy that seems easiest for spirits to take. These will show up in photos as a ball of light, varying in size. Most orbs are not visible at the time the photo was taken.
Dust directly in front of the camera lens can look similar to a spirit orb

Plasmoid

Plasmoids, also known as "Orbs in Motion", are basically orbs that move during the time of camera

Ghost Stories of Delaware County

exposure. They will show up as a short streak of light, or as an orb with a tail, suggesting motion. These are easier to distinguish as not being dust, because they are moving at very high speeds. Most plasmoids are not visible at the time the photo was taken. Some fast falling objects (such as rain drops) can show up looking like plasmoids, though, so don't try to take photos in those types of conditions.

Residual Haunting

Not technically referred to as a haunting, but more of an energy imprint. When a spirit is seen doing the same thing at specific intervals constantly. Perhaps the spirit is trapped repeating a specific moment in life, or perhaps it is just a flash from the past during a traumatic moment in someone's life.

Shadow People

"Shadow People" are exactly what they sound like. They are unexplainable shadows in photographs and video, and sometimes you can even see them with the naked eye. These are believed to be associated with dark entities, possible evil or angry spirits.

Sound Anomaly

Sounds that have no apparent explainable source. This can include, but is not limited to footsteps,

Ghost Stories of Delaware County

knocks, and voices from unseen sources. Sometimes you can't even hear the sound anomaly until you play back recorded audio, similar to EVP.

Temperature Monitors

Temperature are either infrared point and shoot style, or have a hand held probe. Cold and hot spots have been noted to associated with paranormal activity for ages. These monitors can help you measure these spots. Although, it is believed that feeling colder or hotter is actually associated with spirits taking your own heat or adding heat to your body. So, you feel colder or hotter, but you aren't physically colder or hotter. I have felt areas where it feels at least 20 degrees colder, but have never actually measured a temperature difference.

Vortex

Vortices are also technically orbs. A vortex occurs when an orb is moving at a VERY high speed, and streaked all the way across the camera's field of view during exposure. This gives the look of a long streak or funnel, and sometimes can look like a string was held front of the camera lens. This is one of the reasons you shouldn't use camera straps, they can show up looking like a vortex if they get in front of the lens.

•

Ghost Stories of Delaware County

ABOUT THE AUTHOR

The author along Hadrian's Wall, England

Charles J. Adams III

Charles J. Adams III resides in Reading, Pennsylvania. He is the morning air personality on WEEU in Reading and is a travel writer and columnist for the *Reading Eagle* newspaper. Adams has led ghost tours in the United Kingdom, New York City, and other areas and he has served as a consultant or on-camera guest on ghostly topics on the History Channel, The Learning Channel, MTV, and other networks. He has been interviewed about the supernatural for radio, TV, and newspapers across the United States and in several foreign countries. This is his 21st book about ghosts and haunted places.

Ghost Stories of Delaware County

ACKNOWLEDGMENTS

INDIVIDUALS
Jane Viprino, Jen O'Hare, Carol Sollenberger, Lindy Wardell, Helen Thomas, Ann Smith, Laurie Hull, John W. Haigis, Thomas Roy Smith, Dan Diehl

BOOKS
"History of Delaware County," H.G. Ashmead; "Watson's Annals of Philadelphia and Pennsylvania," John F. Watson; "Old Roads Out of Philadelphia," John T. Faris; "Where Pennsylvania History Began," Henry D. Paxson; "Proceedings of the Delaware County Historical Society," "Night Stalks the Mansion,"
Harold Cameron and Constance Westbie;
"The Story of My Childhood," John Bunting

INTERNET SITES
www.delcohistory.org; www.delcoghosts.com; www.ridleytownshiphistory.com; www.piratesinfo.com; www.theshadowlands.net; www.darbyhistory.com; www.PastTimesPresent.com; www.delcotimes.com; www.brandywinecountry.com; www.nstm.net

ORGANIZATIONS
Delaware County Historical Society, Pennsylvania Historical and Museum Commission, Sellers Memorial Library, Indian Echo Caverns, Delaware County Paranormal Research, Parastudy, Inc.; Upper Providence Township, Darby Borough Historical and Preservation Society, Widener University

PERIODICALS
News of Delaware County, The Philadelphia Inquirer, The Daily Times, Philadelphia Magazine, Town Talk

Ghost Stories of Delaware County

ALSO FROM EXETER HOUSE BOOKS
*COAL COUNTRY GHOSTS
(SCHUYLKILL & CARBON COUNTIES, PA.)
✸GHOST STORIES OF CHESTER COUNTY AND THE BRANDYWINE VALLEY
✸MONTGOMERY COUNTY GHOST STORIES
✸BUCKS COUNTY GHOST STORIES
✸PHILADELPHIA GHOST STORIES
✸NEW YORK CITY GHOST STORIES
✸POCONO GHOSTS, LEGENDS & LORE, BOOK I
✸POCONO GHOSTS, LEGENDS & LORE, BOOK II
✸GHOST STORIES OF PITTSBURGH AND ALLEGHENY COUNTY
✸PENNSYLVANIA DUTCH COUNTRY GHOSTS, LEGENDS & LORE
✸GHOST STORIES OF THE LEHIGH VALLEY
✸GHOST STORIES OF THE DELAWARE COAST
✸SHIPWRECKS, SEA STORIES & LEGENDS OF THE DELAWARE COAST
✸GHOST STORIES OF BERKS COUNTY, BOOK I
✸GHOST STORIES OF BERKS COUNTY, BOOK II
✸GHOST STORIES OF BERKS COUNTY, BOOK III
✸BERKS THE BIZARRE
✸LEGENDS OF LONG BEACH ISLAND
✸ CAPE MAY GHOST STORIES, BOOK I
✸CAPE MAY GHOST STORIES, BOOK II
✸CAPE MAY GHOST STORIES, BOOK III
✸SHIPWRECKS & LEGENDS 'ROUND CAPE MAY
ALL TITLES AVAILABLE FOR PURCHASE OR ORDER AT BOOKSTORES OR MAJOR ONLINE BOOKSELLERS
FOR A FREE CATALOG WRITE TO

EXETER HOUSE BOOKS
P.O. BOX 8134, READING, PA 19603
or
www.ExeterHouseBooks.com
Exeter House Books   David J. Seibold, Publisher